The
Christmas
Star

ALSO BY ROBERT TATE MILLER

Secret Santa
Forever Christmas

The
Christmas
Star

A Love Story

ROBERT TATE MILLER

Waterfall
PRESS

Text copyright © 2017 by Robert Tate Miller
All rights reserved.

No part of this book may be reproduced, or stored in a retrieval system, or transmitted in any form or by any means, electronic, mechanical, photocopying, recording, or otherwise, without express written permission of the publisher.

Published by Waterfall Press, Grand Haven, MI

www.brilliancepublishing.com

Amazon, the Amazon logo, and Waterfall Press are trademarks of Amazon.com, Inc., or its affiliates.

ISBN-13: 9781503941342
ISBN-10: 1503941345

Cover design by Shasti O'Leary Soudant

Printed in the United States of America

For Colin

PROLOGUE

"There is only one thing that can destroy darkness—and that is light."

Pastor Joe Moody loved talking about light. It was his favorite Sunday morning topic. I remember so clearly his Christmas Eve sermon the night before the accident. He compared the crucial moments in life to lighthouses.

"Those lighthouse moments are like markers in the mist of memory," Pastor Joe said. "As we look back, they illuminate the path we've walked to the present. That night in Bethlehem was the ultimate lighthouse moment. That was the moment that brought a light to the world that can never be extinguished."

For me, one such moment arrived on a crisp, clear Christmas morning in Manchester, Maine. On that day, my lighthouse came crashing down.

CHAPTER ONE

"Storm's a-coming, Paul. Try and finish up early if you can."

"Sure thing, Ray." I mumbled the words under my breath as I strolled out of the Manchester Post Office, a bloated bag of holiday mail slung over my chafed shoulder. It was early afternoon, and I was beginning my second go-round with my second stuffed postal bag.

Ray Waldrop was the postmaster, my boss, and—as far as I was concerned—an idiot. He knew it was Christmas Eve, knew I was hauling three to four times my usual mail load, and he had to know—if he had a lick of sense—that there was no way on earth I was going to "finish up early." The previous Christmas Eve I'd come in almost ninety minutes behind schedule, and I doubted this year would be any different. The weight of my canvas sack told me so.

At the corner of First and Main, I stopped to check the sky. I could still see a snatch of blue—a hopeful sign. Maybe the storm would hold off until I finished my rounds.

I'd been toting mail for the Manchester PO going on fifteen years, and I'd come to truly despise every step of my daily route. It hadn't always been that way. I'd once been the happy-go-lucky mailman, the guy who knew everybody's name and business. I used to call out greetings as I passed. Sometimes I'd stop in at grandmotherly Eileen Clarke's for lemonade and cookies, or at Red's Barber Shop on the square for the latest scuttlebutt and a bottle of ice-cold cola from his old-timey soda machine. Back then, I walked with a skip in my step and a grin on my face. Life was good then.

Those days were long past. Mail carrying had become a loathsome obligation. A paycheck. Health insurance. I rarely engaged customers anymore and only spoke when spoken to. I wasn't the same man. I'd lost my joie de vivre. My zest for life. My hope.

Four hours later, as I was trudging along Jackson Street, the first flakes fell. Though my load had been lightened considerably by that time, the pain in my shoulder still swelled with the chafing of the strap. From the weight of my bag, I figured I had about a half hour left in my rounds. It was already pitch dark.

I stopped and checked the sky again. A deep gray cloud cover had settled over town, and there wasn't even a wisp of wind. In my experience, stillness was winter's warning. Calm meant snow, and in northern Maine, snow seldom came in moderation. We were going to get socked. Another white Christmas in Manchester.

As if Mother Nature were reading my thoughts, the snow began to fall a little harder. The air was moist, and even though the temperature was hovering around freezing, it felt much colder. "Bone chilling," as my grandfather used to say.

There was a blizzard coming, and the weathercasters predicated a doozy. The greater Manchester area was expecting up to two feet of snow in the next twenty-four hours.

I plodded down Maple Street and cut across the deserted town square. Almost all of the shops had closed, and even the most last-minute of Christmas shoppers had long since scurried home to wrap their treasures.

I paused to get my bearings. The square was eerily empty: dark and desolate, a Christmas Eve ghost town.

I noticed a flash of movement on the other side of the center green, and shifted right for a better view. A shadowy shape huddled in the dark alcove of Walker Sporting Goods. I wondered at first if someone was trying to break in. Then I could see that the shadow was just sitting there—curled up in a ball against the frigid air. A transient, I guessed. Occasionally, a rootless wanderer would pass through Manchester en route to or from the Canadian border.

I hesitated, not sure if I should approach. It could be an escaped criminal waiting for some hapless mailman to shank. The attacker would rifle through my bag, tearing apart Christmas cards looking for money while I bled out in the cold. I smiled at my dark musing, and then a more reasoned thought entered my mind. What if this stranger was injured and needed help? Curiosity won out. I walked over.

"Hello?"

I strained to see into the entryway's dark niche. The stranger looked up at me. As my eyes adjusted, I could see it was a woman. She hugged her knees tightly to her chest and had no coat or hat, no gloves. Her shoes were so ragged and worn she might as well have been barefoot. Her face was weathered and dull, her hands and fingers caked with several layers of dirt. The eyes, though, didn't fit this picture of gloom. They were crystal-clear sky blue, staring out from a grimy face that looked like it hadn't seen a washcloth in weeks. A small tuft of chestnut-colored hair peeked out from beneath an old, worn-out beanie. She spoke in a quivering smoker's voice.

"Merry Christmas."

I fished in my coat pocket for spare change and came out with a handful of lint. I pulled my wallet from my pants. It was empty save for a wrinkled liquor-store receipt. Like so many of the debit generation, I no longer carried cash.

"Sorry," I said. "I don't have any money." She waved me off as if this fact didn't trouble her in the least. "Do you have someplace you can go?" If her answer was no, I wasn't sure what I was going to do.

"I'm right where I need to be," she said.

I thought it was a curious thing to say, and I had no idea what she meant by it. I felt awkward and useless. It was a snowy Christmas Eve, this poor woman was obviously in need, and I hadn't a thing to offer.

"You go on now," she said. "You've got deliveries. Folks need their mail, especially on Christmas."

And of course she was right. There were still a dozen or so houses left on my route, houses no doubt wondering what was keeping their last-minute cards and packages. But it didn't seem right to walk away.

I looked across the square at Charlie's Diner, its shades drawn, the "Closed" sign hanging in the door window. I couldn't even buy her a hot meal. I knew I needed to move on and finish my rounds, but my feet wouldn't cooperate. I felt compelled to do something . . . *anything* for her . . . but I had nothing to offer.

"God loves you," I said and immediately felt foolish. *What a trite and meaningless cliché,* I thought. I'd long stopped believing in God, and I didn't go to church or pray. I felt like a phony uttering such a hopeful and empty sentiment. I waited for the pitiable woman to spit my words back in my face, tell me just how far that *love* had gotten her. Instead, her chapped lips creased into a faint smile.

"I know," she said. "But, my dear Paul, tonight . . . *you* need him more than I do."

I was taken aback. The way she spoke my name—as if she knew me. But I was sure I'd never seen her before in my life. I would have remembered such a face, such penetrating eyes.

"Here," I said. I peeled off my long woolen hand-me-down over-coat. "Take this." A part of me resisted the urge to give away the only thing between me and the bitter cold. It was my favorite coat, one handed down from my father, who'd gotten it from his father. I knew it seemed foolish, but the part of me that needed to help this woman drowned out the voice of reason. I gently draped my old coat around her trembling shoulders. She pulled the cover snugly about her and smiled. Then she raised a frail hand and gestured for me to move in closer, as if she had some confidence to share.

When she spoke, her voice was clear and calm.

"Verily I say unto you, inasmuch as ye have done it unto one of the least of these, my brethren, ye have done it unto me."

◆ ◆ ◆

As I continued up the street, I pondered the woman's words. I knew the quote well: Matthew 25:40. It was one of Rebecca's favorites, and I could almost hear Pastor Joe's voice reciting it from the podium as part of some long-forgotten sermon.

When I reached the next corner, I turned back to look at the strange woman. The storefront alcove was empty. She was gone. I surveyed the square to see if I could spot her. Nothing. She had vanished into thin air. I stood there for a moment, as the wind kicked up and the snow began to fall harder, and wondered where she could have gone so quickly.

There was a strange tingling along my spine and an uneasiness in my stomach. I suddenly felt the tug of the bottle, and along with this feeling of confusion and unease, memories of Megan flashed in my head—my old recurring dark visions. I knew that only drink would dim them.

I must finish my rounds, I thought. *Time to get home, where it's warm.* I pictured where I'd left the bottle, a third full and near the hearth, and realized with a stab of panic the liquor store would be closed tomorrow. Would I have enough? I dreaded the idea of experiencing Christmas Day stone-cold sober.

I turned down Chapel Street and stopped outside Manchester Christian Church. Manchester Christian was one of those old-style New England churches. White on white. Simple and elegant. It had once been my church. As I looked up at the steeple, the chimes began to toll six. I tried to catch a glimpse of ol' Walter, the bell ringer, so that I could toss him a wave. Walter was pushing eighty, and he'd been ringing that bell—every hour on the hour—for over fifty years. Rain or shine, sleet or snow, Walter was at his post. Though his vocation had left him nearly deaf in both ears, he never complained. He loved his job. Walter had no wife or kids or any family that I knew of, but he had his bell and the satisfaction of knowing that—wherever he went in town—he was known as "Walter the bell ringer."

I used to pity him, thinking how sad it was that so little in life could bring a man gratification. Now I envied the old man in the tower. He had found something that would never be mine—contentment.

The church marquee glowed, trumpeting that evening's eight o'clock Christmas Eve service. The massive pipe organ rumbled inside. Helen the organist was warming up. Soon, churchgoers from all over town would file out of their homes and make their way through the falling snow and icy streets to hear Pastor Joe's sermon. Had it been four Christmases past, I would have been among them, walking hand in hand with my wife, Rebecca, and daughters, Megan and Abbey. I would have led them down the aisle, exchanging Christmas greetings with friends and neighbors as we passed.

We'd have slipped into our usual pew, left side, four back from the front. Everybody knew to leave the Bennett family space on the aisle. The girls would have poked and teased each other, and Rebecca would have looked to me to do something. I'd have shrugged as if I hadn't a clue how to rein in a pair of feuding sisters. Rebecca would have shaken her head in mock dismay and put on her serious Mommy voice to bring them into line.

"Girls! Enough."

Manchester Christian had once been a big part of my life, the center of my family's world. No more. I hadn't set foot inside the church since that bleak Wednesday morning four years earlier. The funeral. The second darkest day of my life.

But I've gotten ahead of myself.

CHAPTER TWO

My name is Paul Thomas Bennett, and from as early as I can remember, I have loved stories. Reading them. Hearing them. Making them up. Before I could actually write down my own offbeat creations, I'd find someone willing to listen and give them a good show. Most of the time, my dad was my sounding board. Henry "Hank" Bennett was the Brooklyn cab driver who had raised me on his own after my mom died a few days shy of my fifth birthday. Whenever I had a new story in my hot little hand, I'd make Pops stop what he was doing and give me an audience. My melodramatic tales had me foiling bank robberies, finding rare gold coins, rescuing kittens from the sewer drain, and spying on the aliens that lived two doors down.

By age seven, I was already putting my pencil to good use, scrawling out my chicken-scratched stories on lined paper, filling up a half-dozen loose-leaf notebooks with my fanciful drivel.

I was nine when I decided I should use my developing literary talents to make a little coin. That was the summer I started my own neighborhood business and dubbed it Storytime, Inc. For a dollar, I'd come to your house and read your child a Paul Thomas Bennett original bedtime story. Using my friends' little brothers and sisters as my marketing team, I soon had a handful of regular clients. The parents liked it because they could do other things while I story-told their kids to sleep.

It didn't take me long to realize my little business was actually hard work, especially when my junior clients wanted to pitch in with their own plot twists. I kept my little enterprise up and running for over a year, then got bored with it and closed up shop.

By the time I entered high school, I had three dozen notebooks full of short stories and essays. By then, I was certain how I wanted to spend my life—I was going to be a novelist, and a rich and famous one at that. I'd wander through bookstores and imagine seeing my own name in broad type at the top of a hardcover book. I imagined sitting next to a pretty girl on the subway who was reading my latest book, and surprising her by pointing out that I was—in fact—the author. Of course, she'd be duly impressed, and I'd offer to autograph it for her. A published author. I couldn't imagine there was anything more wonderful in all the world. But that was soon to change.

Maybe my literary dreams were a bit grandiose, but if not for my budding writing talent, I never would have met Rebecca, and the story of that terrible and wonderful Christmas never would have been written.

◆ ◆ ◆

The winter of my junior year in high school, two representatives of Camp Arrowhead for Boys and Girls, a rich kids' camp in the Catskills, stopped by our school to find counselor-in-training candidates.

Only sophomores and juniors with at least a B-plus average and exemplary citizenship were invited to the presentation. At the time, I carried a B-minus average and had spent six hours in detention for various conduct-code violations. However, I would not be denied. I figured I could show up, say that my name was inadvertently left off the list, and nobody would be the wiser. Turned out it was even easier than that. There wasn't even a list.

Two counselors, a clean-cut boy and a prim-and-pretty girl, gave the dozen or so students who'd showed a slick and overcooked sales pitch, and I fell hard. I'd only been out of the city twice in all my seventeen years: once was to Atlantic City with my uncle, and another time to Boston with my dad to see my sick grandmother, who died before we even got there. The promise of a summer in the rolling green hills of upstate New York was so enticing that I determined then and there I was going to land the gig, even if I had to cheat, beg, borrow, or steal. To a boy from Brooklyn, Camp Arrowhead looked like paradise.

When it came time for Q&A, my hand shot up.

"When can I start?" I said.

The counselors smiled. "First, you have to write an essay." I noticed some of the other students casting sideways glances my way. They knew I shouldn't even be in the room, but fortunately, nobody said a word. They probably didn't want to be labeled a snitch in front of their potential summer employers.

I smiled back. "Essay? Sure. I can write an essay."

Essay topic: *Why I Deserve to Be a CIT at Camp Arrowhead.* According to the camp reps, the essay was the most important part of the application. They were playing right into my hands, since I was not one to shy away from a writing assignment. I did a quick mental review of the other students in the room and figured only two were half-decent writers. My chances were better than even money. I decided to give the selection committee a paper to remember.

The Real Question for Camp Arrowhead is: Do YOU Deserve ME?

It was a risky introduction, but I was betting whoever read the essays would be tired of the same ol' clichéd garbage. Once I had them hooked by my pretentious opening line, I hit them with a composition that was witty, refreshingly honest, and even a little touching. I pulled out all the stops and wasn't above playing off my lower-middle-class-raised-by-a-single-dad upbringing to score points.

If you bestow on me one of your coveted CIT slots, I concluded, *I promise to clean the toilets and showers with my toothbrush every night if need be.*

I asked my English teacher, Mrs. Hansen, to look over the essay for errors, did a quick polish, and sent it off.

Three weeks after mailing off the application, my answer came in the afternoon mail. I clutched the envelope in my sweaty hands for a good ten minutes, staring at the embossed "Camp Arrowhead" lettering. I was petrified to peel back the flap and learn my summer fate. If they'd said no, I'd be washing dishes at the Elks Club or tearing movie tickets at the dollar theater. Summer in the city was hot and sweaty and suffocating. The heat reflecting off the buildings made it feel like you were living in a microwave. Every alternative seemed depressing after glimpsing the holy grail of summer jobs.

It was Pops' gentle urging that finally prompted me to rip the envelope apart.

"C'mon, Paul. I want to see if I'm losing my partner in crime this summer."

I tore into the letter, my heart racing, my stomach one big nervous knot. And there it was in my trembling hand—as clear as a blue mountain lake. Paul Thomas Bennett of Argyle Road in Brooklyn would spend the summer of his seventeenth year in paradise. At the time, all I could think about was sun and canoes and pretty girls. I had no idea that job was the first step on a long journey, one that would one day bring me to the icy sidewalk on a snowy Christmas Eve in Manchester, Maine.

CHAPTER THREE

To be honest, I can't say I remember seeing Rebecca around camp before that fateful afternoon in August. There were over four hundred campers at Arrowhead, and I spent most of my time on the boys' side. I was assigned to the Woodchuck Cabin, made up of nine-year-old terrors with limitless energy and a propensity for wreaking havoc. I led hikes, supervised cabin cleanup, helped run the nightly bonfire, worked in the arts-and-crafts building, and assisted the lifeguards down at the waterfront. I loved every minute of it. When the wake-up bell rang every morning, I would jump down from my top bunk ready to roll. I marched my little campers around like a field general leading his troops into battle. I quickly learned that it was to my advantage to wear the little imps down to such a degree that by the end of the night, they would collapse onto their bunks in total exhaustion.

I crossed paths often with the older girl campers, but I was usually too busy keeping the Woodchuckers under my firm control to pay much notice. As a rule, counselors were forbidden from socializing with (much less dating) the campers—but there wasn't any specific rule about CITs. A number of my fellow junior counselors took full advantage of the loophole, some of them lining up summer romances within a few hours of arriving at camp. But there was precious little time in my schedule to think about a summer girlfriend. And as I'd never before had a girlfriend, summer or otherwise, I wasn't really sure how to obtain one or how to play the dating game once procurement of said girlfriend had taken place.

I soon found that my embarrassing lack of experience with the fairer sex was not the only thing separating me from my CIT counterparts. Most of them, like the campers, were from wealthy families. They'd grown up in places that ended with "Hill," like Carnegie Hill and Cobble Hill. They went to schools with elitist names like Dalton, Riverdale, and Trinity. They'd soon head off to Ivy League futures and trust funds and perfect lives. I had a wholly different childhood experience.

The years of my boyhood were broken into two acts: *before* my mother died and *after* my mother died. Unlike most of the plays on Broadway (that I could never afford), the first act was shorter than the second. And as the years passed, the first-act scenes seemed to grow murkier and murkier until the mental images of my mother melded with my dreams of her. After a time, I wasn't sure what really happened and what was part of a five-year-old's imagination. I dreamed of her often in the months just after her passing. So many years later, I still have vague pictures of her as young and pretty and vibrant, and sometimes I'll hear a woman laugh and think how it sounds a bit like my mother's laugh.

By the time I reached adulthood, any recollections of Mom were few and fleeting, and of those few memories, most were of her sick and in bed and weak. I can still see myself sitting on the edge of her bed, gently holding her cool, gray hand, waiting for her to open her eyes so I could tell her about my day at school. I remember her head wrapped in a daisy-print scarf and wondering why her hair had fallen out, afraid that mine would suffer a similar fate.

The day Mom died it was raining, a hard and cold late autumn rain, and I remember staring out her bedroom window as my father said goodbye to her. He later told me that he'd done everything to keep me out of the room, but I'd insisted on being with him. I was afraid to be alone, afraid that I might die, too. I'd had a dream a few nights earlier that my mother had come into my room and told me she was taking me with her to heaven. I'd sat up in bed screaming like my arm had been cut off. Pops had come running to find me trembling and inconsolable. He had to take me down to the kitchen for some midnight ice cream to settle me down.

My dad later told me that in her final moments my mother had called for me, but I'd stayed by the window. At the time, he figured it was my nightmare that made me keep my distance. He'd wanted to bring me over to her, but my mother had stopped him.

"Let him be," she said. "I know he loves me, and that's all that matters."

"I think you were just afraid," Pops told me years later. "Afraid that if you said goodbye, she'd think it was okay to go, and you'd never see her again."

For a long time after she died, I didn't speak of my mother at all. My dad said that once he was in the kitchen fixing lunch with the window open, and I was playing outside in the yard with a neighborhood friend. "The friend asked you a question," Pops said. "He asked if you missed your mother. Your answer was heartbreaking. You said, 'I don't have a mother,' and kept right on playing.

"I remember that I broke down sobbing right then and there. I got the sandwiches soggy with my tears and had to start over. For the longest time, you pretended she was a figment of your imagination. Then, one day, when you were ten years old—it was raining real hard—and you looked at me and said in a very matter-of-fact way, 'It's raining on a Tuesday—just like when Mom died.'"

From then on, I would bring up my mother from time to time, ask questions about her, some of them inane and others more profound.

"I knew someday you'd probably want to have a heart-to-heart," Pops said, "and that I'd better be ready. And then one night, out of the blue, I was right. *Pops, do you think Mom still remembers me?*"

My dad told me he was standing in the doorway of my bedroom when I asked him that question. His hand was on the light switch, and he'd just bid me good night. I was twelve years old. He was tired from driving his taxi and really wasn't in the mood. He knew, however, that he couldn't walk away from it. Even years later, I still recall watching him from my bed, wondering what he was thinking. I clearly remember what I was thinking—that part of me wanted him to give me the safe answer, tell me that of course she remembered me, that she was probably looking down on me at that very moment. But my dad was a deeply honest man, and not skilled at weaving tales designed for comfort's sake. My question obviously moved him, and he took a moment to gather himself, walked over, and sat down on the edge of my bed. I stared at him, my stomach tied up in knots, not sure I really wanted to hear what he had to say.

"Son, I sure wish I knew," Pops said. "The life we live here is mystery enough; the life that comes after is beyond my comprehension. I'd like to tell you *yes*, but I think you know I'd be hypothesizing about something that greater minds than mine have been speculating on for thousands of years. I don't know what comes after—or even if there is an *after*.

"But, I'll tell you what I do know. There are times that I can hear and feel your mother so clearly it's as if she's right next to me. Sometimes, her presence is so strong I can almost smell her perfume. She always wore Charlie—just a light spray, enough to drive me crazy. So I don't know what that says, or if it means anything at all, but if I were a betting man, I'd bet that there is something out there, some place that's invisible to us mere mortals. And if there is such a place, Mom has to be there, and I hope it's as nice and pretty as you might picture heaven to be. And if she's there in this place, then my best guess is . . . she remembers you, and she loves you still and always will."

I believed my dad. My dad never lied.

◆ ◆ ◆

There were just under two weeks of camp left when the storm hit. Actually, calling it a storm is a bit of an understatement. It was a rage, a wild, squalling tempest the likes of which I'd never seen. I thought it might just kill us all.

It was a few minutes after four o'clock on that early August afternoon when the dark black clouds blew in from the west. The violent winds kicked up so suddenly there was scarcely enough time to sound the warning bell before the squall exploded in full-force fury.

I was in the arts-and-crafts cabin helping a counselor named Gary run a lanyard-making class when the sudden speedy ping of raindrops on the tin roof startled us to silence. The growing intensity of the impacts told me that it was more than just rain.

"Hail," I whispered. Gary nodded.

Then a flash and a deafening thunderclap.

Gary turned pale. "Nobody panic!"

During counselor training week, all members of the staff had been given specific jobs to perform in the event of a storm. I was part of the dock crew in charge of clearing and securing the waterfront. That meant I had to help ensure everybody was out of the water and all the canoes and paddleboats were pulled up on the beach and upended. In other words, I had to get out in it.

Soon, the hail-rain was smacking the roof so hard it stared to vibrate. I hurried to the window. Midafternoon looked like midnight; the winds were so strong the metal trash cans were rolling around like tumbleweed. Garbage blustered across the grounds.

As the warning bell clanged, the precamp training I thought I'd never have to use kicked in. While Gary huddled with the campers in a corner of the cabin, I bolted from arts and crafts out into the deluge and sprinted down the slippery hillside to the dock.

I was first on the scene and wondered if the rest of the team had taken one look out the window and decided to take a pass. But then another CIT named Marty arrived, followed by senior counselor Jim, who pointed across the storm-tossed lake and briefed us on the situation.

"The bugs are on the water."

The Ladybugs, a couple dozen of Arrowhead's littlest girl campers, were returning from a canoe trip across the lake. I could see their mini canoe fleet about twenty yards offshore. By the time I arrived at the beach, the powerful wind gusts were pitching the Ladybug canoes about like tops in the ocean. I could see the girls out on the waves, frozen with fear. Some were crying out for help, while others were just crying.

"We have to get them out now!" Jim shouted over the gale-force winds.

I was scared. This was the first time in my life I'd ever been in real danger. And the part of me that was terrified out of my wits did battle with the part that was thoroughly loving the excitement of it all. It was a dangerous rush that I'd never experienced before.

I did my best to suppress my fears as I plunged into the roiling water. I waded out knee-deep, grabbed onto one of the bobbing canoes, and pulled it to shore. By that time, two more CITs and another counselor had joined us. They plunged in with me and together we battled the elements to haul the rest of the Ladybugs to safety.

"It's going to be okay," I said to a canoe filled with petrified girls. I had no idea if I was right. As I watched the little girls trembling and white with fear, my heart went out to them. I said a quick little prayer that was scarcely a prayer at all.

Help me comfort them.

Then, as if it had been instantly downloaded into my head, I remembered a silly song we taught the little kids first week of camp. I started singing, and a few of the Ladybugs joined in.

> I'm a little acorn brown, lying on the cold,
> cold ground. Everybody steps on me! That is
> why I'm cracked, you see! I'm a nut-t-t! I'm a
> nut! I'm a nut! I'm a nut-t-t!

As I helped lug the last canoe up onto the sand, a lightning strike cracked so loud and close it made every hair on my body stand. My ears rang, and for a moment, I thought it was over; I was on my way to meet the maker I'd just been praying to. Then, as if a hatch had been pulled back from the sky, hail the size of golf balls pelted us. The little girls screamed and whimpered as three female counselors who'd run down to help us quickly ferried them to shelter, doing their best to shield their little bodies from the icy barrage.

In less than five minutes, our waterfront team had evacuated the Ladybugs from the canoes and ushered them inside to the safety of the main pavilion. I looked around. Jim and I were the only ones left. The senior counselor cupped his hands over his mouth and shouted at me.

"Upend the canoes and get inside!"

I quickly moved from canoe to canoe, flipping them upside down on the sand as the stinging hail pinged off the metal boats and pelted me. When the last boat was secure, I noticed I was the only one left outside. I turned and sprinted up the hill, nearly taking a nosedive on the slick grass. About twenty yards short of the pavilion, I stopped dead in my tracks.

I heard something.

A cry. A wail. It was so slight and weak that, at first, I was almost certain I had imagined it. Then, I heard a faint whimper carried on the wind. I jerked my head around, searching. There was nobody in sight. Again it came, and this time I was sure it was of human origin and coming from the lake. I looked across the wildly rippling water. Still nothing. Then it hit me—another idea that flashed in my mind as if dropped there by some unseen force. There were supposed to be *seven* canoes in all. In my haste to get out of the storm, I had neglected to count. I ran back to the shore and did a quick survey.

Six.

My gut knotted up. Where was number seven? I scanned the water again. There was no boat. Where could it be? Then, another cry.

I must be hearing things. Please, God. Let me be hearing things.

"There's someone out there."

I turned toward the voice. It belonged to a girl camper standing a few feet away, staring at me. She was tall and skinny and looked to be about my age, her flame red hair tied back in a ponytail. She had hazel eyes and a heart-shaped face, and she was sopping wet from head to tail, her soaked Camp Arrowhead T-shirt clinging to her like flypaper. She seemed strangely oblivious to the howling winds and pounding rain and hail. I thought I recognized her from the dining hall, though I didn't know her name. She was staring out at the water. Then she pointed, stretching her whole arm toward the water.

"There! Behind the diving platform!"

A small floating dock hovered about thirty yards offshore. I didn't see anything. I dusted off my authoritative voice and shouted over the rainstorm. "You need to get back inside!" I grabbed her by a bony arm and tried to pull her in the right direction. She was surprisingly strong, and as she jerked away from my grip, a thunderclap burst so loud it made my ears ring like a church bell. The girl didn't flinch.

"It's the rules!" I said. "Now go!"

"Go read your rule book if you want," she said. "I'm going to go get her."

I watched with a mixture of terror and fascination as the redheaded girl ran down the hill, sprinted across the dock, and dove into the raging waters.

I stood on the bank, frozen with indecision. I couldn't believe what had just happened. Was she crazy?

I shouted a feeble "Hey!" and looked back up toward the pavilion. Had anyone else seen? Was anyone coming to help? What was I supposed to do? The junior counselor training hadn't covered such a situation. I could see the crazy chick flailing, her scrawny arms churning furiously through the seething waters. *She's not going to make it to that dock,* I thought. *She's going to die out there.*

My heart raced as my dad's voice whispered in my thoughts. *It's time for action, son. You can figure out the rest later.*

And so I acted, though I had no real purpose or plan. I ran down to the end of the dock and grabbed the ring buoy from the hook. Who was I kidding? I'd never be able to get a good toss in that squally wind. Besides, the foolhardy camper didn't look like she needed help. Even if I did manage to get it near her, she'd likely just swim past it.

And then I heard it, a whisper on the wind, two words faint but clear and undaunted by the roar of the storm.

Go in.

Those were the last two words I wanted to hear at that moment. I so wanted to question the mysterious voice, hoping maybe I'd misunderstood. Then I heard it again. *Go in.* I thought about ignoring the suggestion. It seemed such a fool's errand, a pointless suicidal exercise in futility.

While I stood on the bank debating with myself, the red-haired girl was halfway to the floating dock, plowing through the water with all her might as the storm and wind conspired to swallow her up. And as I looked out over the waves, a flash of green and a glint of silver bobbed into view—the bow of an overturned canoe. The crazy girl was right. There was a Ladybug stranded out there, obscured by the platform, clinging for dear life.

"Wait for me!" I said. *Wait for me?* I thought. *Have I lost my marbles? I'm not that good of a swimmer.* I looked back up the hill one last time, tossed the buoy aside, and plunged into the lake.

CHAPTER FOUR

With the wisdom that years and hindsight bring, I've sometimes wondered if God used inclement weather to herald imminent change in my life. My mother left me on a dark and rainy day, and it was in the rain when another someone arrived, as if God had decided to balance the scales on the stormy afternoon she showed up.

The redheaded girl from the lake was named Rebecca Anne Waverly. She was seventeen years old, all angles, and from a wealthy Manhattan family. Her mother, Jane, was a novelist of the indie variety; her father, Jack, the owner of the prestigious Waverly Art Gallery on Fifth Avenue.

Despite her blue blood, Rebecca didn't have a fleck of self-importance. She was sassy, down to earth, and full of curiosity about the strange and random phenomenon we call life. She was just "Becca" and would forever after be the most heroic person I'd ever met. Although, whenever I called her a hero for her dramatic lake rescue, she'd scoff and accuse me of diminishing the word for the *real* heroes.

"I'm a book nerd who likes to paint landscapes," she once said. "Please don't make me out to be more than I am."

The midteenage version of Rebecca was charmingly awkward, with black-rimmed glasses and that delightfully frizzy red hair. The head turner she would become had yet to show up, and the entire summer might have passed without me noticing her at all—save for the fact we saved a life together. Actually, Becca did most of the saving, and I was always quick to correct anyone who tried to paint the rescue as a joint effort. I was just along for the ride.

After the rescue of the stranded Ladybug, Rebecca and I were suddenly camp heroes. Bound by our dramatic shared experience, we started hanging out together during our free time, thumbing our noses at the "no fraternization" rule. At first, our friendship was strictly platonic, but soon camp tongues were wagging with news that Becca and Paul were a couple, even though we didn't see ourselves that way.

"What are we?" I said one evening as we sat knee to knee and dangled our toes off the end of the dock.

"Acquaintances," Becca said.

"Oh," I said.

For some reason I was too naïve to understand why her answer hurt. Rebecca must have sensed the disappointment in my tone because she immediately gave us an upgrade.

"Friends."

Friends, I thought. *That's fine.* The dawning of our relationship consisted of a few strolls in the woods and shared s'mores by the campfire. There were no romantic fireworks, no stolen kisses, and no starry-eyed protestations of devotion. It just seemed natural. Comfortable.

In those early days, when I was first getting to know her, Rebecca struck me as a little reserved and standoffish, but soon her satirically crisp sense of humor bubbled to the surface. She was well read, loved to draw and paint, and until she came to camp, had never slept a night away from home. And she had striking hazel eyes. When I commented on them one evening as we nestled together on the wooden seat of a rope swing, she rolled them at me.

"Stop it," she said. "I know I'm not pretty, so you don't have to say that."

"Agreed," I said. She glared at me, more amused than hurt. "You're beautiful."

Rebecca flushed and looked away. I wanted to tell her I thought she was the most beautiful girl I'd ever seen, but I sensed that would be coming on a smidge too strong.

We held hands for the first time the last night of camp, slow danced at the farewell party, and shared a sweet and innocent first kiss on the pier beneath the moonlight—near the spot where we'd first met.

When we said goodbye at the buses the next morning, I penned her address on my palm and promised to write. I could tell from the look on her face she had her doubts I would follow through, but by the time the bus dumped me back in Brooklyn, I'd already written a week's worth of *Dear Rebecca* letters. I filled her in on every minute detail of my entire six-hour bus ride sitting next to Freddie "Body Odor" McGraw. Five days after mailing Rebecca my camp-bus missives, I got a week's worth of letters in return. I eagerly devoured every word of her artistic handwriting. After I'd read the last one for the third time and tucked the wrinkled papers in the top drawer of my dresser, I looked in the mirror and smiled. I had a secret that made my inexperienced heart leap in my chest.

◆　◆　◆

"Pops, I think I might be in love."

Pops and I were shooting hoops at the schoolyard a block from our house. It was another weekend ritual we'd started not long after Mom died, back when I was so young and small I couldn't even get the ball up to the bottom of the net. As the years passed and I grew into a teen, shooting baskets with Pops was still something I looked forward to far more than I let on.

"Oh, yeah?" Pops said. He put up one of his patented hook shots that clanged off the front of the rim. He was an expert at feigning non-chalance, acting as if my declaration held no more importance than me commenting on the weather or the previous night's Knicks game.

"Name's Rebecca." I scooped up the ball and executed a fadeaway jumper from ten feet. Nothing but chain net. "You know—the girl I met at camp."

"Oh, right. The one who sent you all those letters."

"Yeah. That one." I retrieved yet another of my dad's errant shots.

"Where's she from again?" he asked. I knew that he knew. He'd seen the return address on her letters, and my father never missed a detail.

I whipped him a crisp pass. "Carnegie Hill."

"Nice neighborhood."

I wondered if he was being passive aggressive about where Rebecca lived. I chose to ignore it. He dribbled the ball behind his back and lost control.

"Yeah," I said. "Nice girl, too."

Pops took a shot that rolled around the rim and went in. He winked at me. "She's got good taste in boys."

And that was it. He didn't ask me anything else, and I didn't volunteer any details. He didn't try to make any clichéd point about us being from different worlds, not even a veiled reference to her wealth and my poverty. I knew he was curious, but he was giving me space, letting me open up in my own time. I appreciated that, but a part of me wanted the fatherly press conference. I was eager to talk about Rebecca. I was thrilled and giddy and terrified. For me, love was virgin territory. I had nothing on my romantic résumé to show my readiness for something so life shattering, and I wanted my dad to ask me about all those things. Maybe I just wanted an excuse to say Rebecca's name. But he held his tongue.

"I need to cut our game short this morning," I said. I took a three-pointer that banged off the metal backboard.

Pops gave me a sly grin. "You're meeting your girl, aren't you?"

"Becca, I told my dad about us."

The morning we said goodbye at camp, we'd made a pact we wouldn't see each other for a month. Even though we lived a mere borough away, we agreed to spend that time apart so we could see what it felt like to miss one another. Actually, it was Rebecca's idea, and I only went along with it so I wouldn't seem too desperate and eager. I knew what she was doing. She wanted to see if we were more than a summer fling—if I was really and truly interested in her.

Day after day I drew an X on my calendar—slowly marking off the days until our reunion. So many times I picked up the phone, gripped it tightly, and made excuses for why one little call wouldn't be breaking our promise. But I'd always find a way to resist the temptation. *Thirty days,* I reminded myself again and again. *It's just thirty days.* I imagined Rebecca calmly waiting out the hiatus without so much as a single temptation to call or write. I'd later find out she was just as anxious as I had been, and that she had come close to breaking the "no contact" pact on the very night she arrived home from camp.

The month-long hiatus lasted exactly nine days. The Saturday after the first week of our senior year in high school, being without Rebecca Waverly became simply more than my young heart could bear. I called her and told her I had to see her or I was going to spontaneously combust. I was stunned by her response, which showed exactly how little I knew about women.

"What took you so long?"

Becca was sitting on the wall at Bethesda Fountain in Central Park when I walked up. I could tell from her expression she was trying her best not to appear too excited to see me. But her lovely hazel eyes gave her away. There was no crazy embrace, no kisses on the cheek, not even a handshake. I just sat beside her like we'd never been apart.

She smiled when she heard I'd told my dad about her. "Wow. What did he say?"

"Not much. I could tell he was happy, though."

"That's great," Rebecca said. There was a tinge of awkwardness between us that I desperately wanted to go away. The days apart and the unfamiliar environment had diluted the easy familiarity we'd had at camp.

"What about your parents?" I said. "What did they say?" Rebecca looked at me and didn't answer, and I felt my heart sink a little. "You didn't tell them, did you?" She shook her head. "Becca, why not? Are you ashamed of me or something?"

"Paul, no!" she said. "I just don't want to deal with them." She took my hand, and my heart skipped. I felt better.

"What do you mean?" I asked, though all I was thinking about was how warmly perfect her hand felt in mine.

"They'll make a big deal out of it," she said. "They'll pretend like it's an issue."

I looked at her, genuinely perplexed. "Like *what's* an issue?" She gazed at me like a worldly-wise teacher at a naïve student. I pulled my hand away. We'd only been back together five minutes, and we were already fighting.

"Paul, please don't. It's just . . . they're not like me. They're very narrow about certain things."

"What *things*?" I said.

"Just our differences," she said. The usually cool and confident Rebecca was searching for the right words and not finding them.

"You mean the fact that I'm poor and you're rich?" I said, my stomach tightening. It was the elephant in the room, the thing that, deep down, I feared most. She looked at me with her hazel eyes. I wanted her to correct me, to tell me I had it all wrong. Instead, I got a woeful look, and then those lovely eyes clouded up. I was right, and she knew I was right, but she couldn't bring herself to admit it.

"Fine," I said. Though I knew it wasn't her fault, I was hurt and angry. She was just trying to spare my feelings. I stood up, ready to beat a hasty retreat. My heart was thumping, my cheeks flushed. I needed to find a place where I could sob in private—where I could grieve the tragic end of my short and sweet first love. I started to speak, but Becca was up and right in front of me, invading my space. She took my face in her hands and forced me to look at her.

"Paul, stop. You know I care about you."

"Do I, Rebecca? Do I know?" It was a line I'd seen in a movie and had unconsciously stored away to bootleg one day. She removed her hands from my face, and I could tell I'd hurt her.

"Well, if you don't believe in us . . ." she said. I felt like a huge jerk. She'd flipped the script on me.

"No, Becca. I do. I think you should be honest with them. They're going to find out about me sooner or later. Right?"

Rebecca nodded and kissed me on the cheek. "You're right. You're so right. Come on!" She took me by the hand and pulled me with her.

"Where are we going?" I said.

"My house."

◆　◆　◆

"Mother, Father, I'd like you to meet Paul Thomas Bennett. Paul, may I present Jack and Jane Waverly."

I was standing in the living room of the Waverlys' lavish, exquisitely decorated apartment. There were Persian rugs and golden fixtures and really expensive artwork and everything else that was totally foreign to my blue-collar Brooklyn existence. I felt like a plastic fork in a china cabinet. Rebecca's formal introduction didn't help. I wondered if her parents insisted on being addressed as "Mother" and "Father."

Jack and Jane Waverly smiled and shook my hand, but they weren't pleased at the sight of this run-of-the-mill chap planting his cheap shoes on their expensive wood floors. I imagined what they were thinking.

Jack, we never should have sent our perfect daughter to summer camp.

You're so right, Jane. Look at the trash she picked up.

"Where are you from, Paul?"

Though Jane Waverly's tone was polite and polished, I could feel the chill. The neighborhood I knew and loved and grew up in suddenly felt like an albatross around my neck. My block was about to stand up to prosecutorial scrutiny—and probably wasn't going to pass muster.

"He's from Brooklyn," Becca said. The *Wanna make something of it?* was implied in her tone.

I smiled at her. "I can speak for myself, you know." I suddenly felt my ears blush. It was a mixture of embarrassment and anger that I was being judged and measured based on my zip code.

Rebecca blushed, and I noticed a twinkle in her dad's eyes. *Maybe he's an ally,* I thought wishfully. "Argyle Road," I said, deciding they needed a more precise location, as if that might somehow lessen the shame of my inferior Brooklyn upbringing. I saved them the trouble of their next two questions. "My mother's dead. My dad drives a cab." They didn't need to know that he was also a part-time custodian.

"*Owns* his own cab," Becca said.

I felt a tinge of pique. She was trying to make me look better. Her response had a ring of desperation, and I knew she'd have to do a lot better than that. Maybe if he owned his own cab company—or several cab companies.

The brief and awkward parental meeting lasted all of ten minutes. Becca saw me off outside the Waverlys' palatial brownstone. I could feel their judgmental eyes on us from the window above. I was more humiliated than angry, and I blamed her for it.

"Rebecca, I didn't need you to sell me to your parents."

"Paul, I wasn't . . . I wouldn't . . ."

"I am who I am, Becca. I'm not going to change. If my poverty is going to be an issue, then maybe we should break up right now."

"Paul . . ." Rebecca took my hands, and again I felt a rush of warmth run through me. Her touch had a disarming power that I knew I'd never be able to resist. "No," she said. Her tone was firm, her eyes resolute. "I love who you are. Everything about you. I love . . . you."

I forgot what I was going to say. Really? She *loved* me? This wealthy, beautiful, perfect girl was in love with regular old lower-middle-class, run-of-the-mill me? I wanted to believe her. I so wanted to believe her, but what if all I represented was a sheltered rich girl thumbing her nose at her imperious parents? What if she was using me to needle them?

"Do *you* . . . love . . . me?" Her voice cracked, her hands trembling in mine. And it dawned on me. She was afraid, too. This amazing, extraordinary girl was afraid I didn't feel the same. I left her hanging so I could bask in that moment of discovery an instant longer.

"Yeah," I said. "Of course I love you. I think I fell in love with you the first moment I saw you. By the lake that day. In the rain." And as I said it, I realized it was true. I fell in love with Rebecca that day at camp in the hailstorm, soaking wet and terrified, the moment she defied my orders and plunged into the churning waters, the day she taught me the meaning of courage. She smiled at me and wiped a tiny tear from just below her left eye.

"Okay then," she said. "Glad that's settled. So, I guess it doesn't matter what my parents think."

Love. The idea seemed too grand to be encapsulated by a mere four letters—a concept altogether ethereal and transcendental, something that should be reserved for those more discerning and experienced. It scared me and thrilled me, but mostly, it made me feel light and invincible. It was as if all the moments and feelings and thoughts of my entire life were preambles to that magnificent revelation. I loved and was loved in return, and all the doubts and ambiguity I'd had about the existence of God vanished. God *had* to exist for something as extraordinary as love to exist. He just had to.

Rebecca was my first love. And even in those heady early days when love was new, I had an inkling she would also be my last.

CHAPTER FIVE

As we navigated our way through our respective senior years of high school, Becca and I tried to spend every free moment together. With our busy schedules, there were precious few of those moments. Our schools were as diverse as our upbringings. Rebecca went to the elite all-girls Brearley School on East Eighty-Third Street, and I went to the not-so-elite PS 369 on State Street in Brooklyn. If Brearley was the Ritz-Carlton of schools, PS 369 was Motel 6. Her private school had everything a wealthy Manhattan debutante could ever desire. Brearley graduates went on to Princeton, Harvard, and Yale. Our graduates went on to McDonald's, Taco Bell, and Kmart.

On Tuesday evenings, Rebecca and I would meet up to study at the stately old New York Public Library. We'd stake out a corner and sit holding hands, noses in our respective books. She'd be in her Brearley blue-and-white uniform, me in my jeans and T-shirt. At the end of the evening, we'd set up our weekend plans, which almost always revolved around our very limited budget. I was broke most of the time, and Rebecca's parents had cut her allowance as a kind of economic sanction to protest our relationship. They figured if we couldn't afford to do anything fun, then we'd soon grow bored of our fledgling romance—or at least Rebecca would. They no doubt pictured her tooling around with highbrow boys from Browning or Trinity.

The Waverlys' fiscal squeeze had the opposite effect. Becca and I became wildly creative at making our own fun on the cheap. Sometimes, we'd meet in Central Park and just walk and talk, while at other times we'd sneak into the movies or stroll around Times Square pretending to be tourists.

I simply loved being near her. When we were apart too long I'd become anxious and moody. Seeing Becca's smile, hearing her lovely lilting voice, or getting a whiff of her fragrance was my only cure. There was just something about Rebecca that made me feel at peace. Every moment away from her was spent in anticipation of when I'd be with her again.

My life had become one big green room, and Rebecca Waverly was the show.

◆ ◆ ◆

"I'm going to ask Rebecca to marry me."

I said the words aloud to myself in the shower one Sunday morning and repeated them to my dad at breakfast. He responded with his usual "nothing rattles me" unflappability, buttering his toast and fishing around a bit.

"Wow. That's a big step."

"I love her, Pops. And she loves me."

I waited for him to tell me we were much too young and inexperienced. Instead, he veered into a story about how he met and wooed my mom.

"Falling in love with your mother did not come in one big dramatic light-bulb moment," Pops said. "It was a gradual dawning: like a sunrise in super slow motion."

It was Pops' favorite story. He told it at least once a year and upon request. His face always lit up at the telling, and I noticed over time that he added flourishes and embellishments that I'm sure he felt kept the story fresh.

◆ ◆ ◆

The first time I saw your mother, it was just after sunset on a sweltering day in mid-July. The time of day they call the magic hour. I was out on the sidewalk tinkering with an old beat-up Indian motorcycle I'd dragged out of a nearby junkyard. I reached up to wipe my forehead with the back of my hand, and that's when I saw her. Claire had just come outside and was sitting on the top step. She and her dad had moved into the row house across the street only a few days earlier. She had a glass of lemonade in one hand, a drawing pad in the other, and a stubby little pencil tucked behind one ear. She was wearing a baby-blue top and tan shorts. She was barefoot and, in the deep purple light of dusk, glowed like an angel. I loved her in an instant.

But the feeling was not mutual.

It was like I was a leper. I did everything I could to win her over, but even though we lived right across the street from one another and went to the same high school, she treated me like I was a total stranger, not even worth a smile or a nod hello. So after several months of the cold treatment, I gave up. I figured if Claire MacDonald didn't think I was worthy of her time, then she wasn't worthy of mine. By that time, she had a boyfriend—a good-looking senior. Popular. Football player. So I wrote her off.

But it's a funny thing about your mother. After I'd written off my chances and stopped acting like a desperate fool, she started becoming a bit friendlier to me. Never could figure out women. She said hello when we passed in the halls at school. She'd sometimes call across the street to ask me about a test or homework or what I was doing with my motorcycle. I'd give her short answers and move on. I wanted her to know that she no longer held sway over me.

Well, the school year whizzed by, and before we knew it, prom was upon us. Being a junior, I'd never been to one before, and I had no intention of ever going—I wasn't a prom kind of guy. But then my buddy Sam came to me, hat in hand, and pitched me an idea.

He wanted me to take his little sister, Michelle, a sophomore who desperately wanted to go because her two best sophomore friends both had prom dates with older guys. Naturally, I refused. Michelle was a spoiled brat, and she'd been nothing but nasty to me ever since I'd known her.

"C'mon," Sam said. "You owe me."

"What do I owe you for?"

I watched as Sam searched his mind for a little something he might have done for me along the way. "Maybe you don't owe me, but I'll owe you—if you do this."

"No, thanks," I said.

"My dad'll give you twenty bucks."

Now back then twenty bucks was a good bit of money, especially for a seventeen-year-old kid. However, I was still on the fence about being a prom date for hire until Sam assured me that to Michelle, I was nothing more than a ticket to the dance. He put me on the phone with his little sister to let her close the deal.

"Don't flatter yourself," Michelle said. "As soon as we walk through the gym doors, I'm going to ditch you to hang out with my friends. You don't even have to take me home."

Michelle was true to her word. A moment after we walked in the gym that prom night, me in my late father's hand-me-down light-blue tuxedo, she in her sister's hand-me-down party dress, she flitted off to find her girlfriends. I heaved a sigh of relief and patted the twenty spot in my pants pocket. Sam was taking Michelle home at the end of the night, so I could leave early. Easiest twenty I ever made.

As I looked around the crowded dance floor that night, my mind drifted to Claire. "How Deep is Your Love" was playing, and I half expected to see her there on the floor draped all over her jock boyfriend, slow dancing on the school logo. When I couldn't spot them, I felt a wave of relief. I didn't want her to see me so pathetic and alone, a pseudo date for some snot-nosed sophomore.

I scooped a glass of punch from the eats table, and one sip told me it had already been spiked. I smiled, looked around, took another sip, and poured it back. Then I saw her. The Bee Gees ended, and the dance floor emptied, clearing my line of vision. Claire was sitting on the third row of the bleachers. She was all by herself, wearing a pretty green dress, her hair up in a bun, her lips bright red, and her makeup flawless. I watched her, her gaze darting around the darkened gym.

Who was I kidding? I'd never really gotten over her. She was still the loveliest girl I'd ever seen. At that moment, I knew good and well that I never would get over Claire MacDonald. She was the only girl that made my heart skip a beat.

I watched her for a moment, so small and lonely, staring out across the gym. I looked around for her boyfriend, figuring he'd stepped away for a minute, but much to my delight, he was nowhere to be seen. I thought what a fool he was—if Claire had been my prom date, I wouldn't have let her out of my sight for a second.

When she spotted me, there was no reaction at first. We looked at each other like Tony and Maria across that crowded dance floor in West Side Story. Finally, she smiled, and I smiled back. Then she waved me over.

"Where's whatshisname?" *I said. She shrugged.*

"Off getting drunk with his friends."

I grinned. "So, you've been ditched?"

"Well, you don't have to look so happy about it," *she said. But she wasn't angry. She seemed almost relieved.* "Get Down Tonight" *by KC and the Sunshine Band started up. Claire brightened.* "Wanna dance?"

"I don't dance," *I said.*

"C'mon, please. I'd like to have at least one dance before I go home."

"No, thanks," *I said.* "Well, good night." *I headed for the door without waiting for a response. It felt great to be in control.*

"Hey, Hank. Wait . . ." *Claire caught up to me.* "Where are you going?"

That was the first time she'd ever said my name. "Home," I said. "To be honest, I don't even want to be here."

"Where's your date?" she asked.

"No idea," I said.

Claire smiled. "So, I guess we're both members of the ditched-by-dates club."

"Guess so," I said. I wasn't about to tell her that my date was actually a paid gig.

"Well . . ." Claire said, "if you won't dance with me, will you at least walk me home?"

The rain started about a block into our seven-block journey home. It was a slow and steady rain, and Claire didn't seem to mind, so I figured I didn't either. She walked in her bare feet, carrying her party shoes in one hand. We walked slowly and leisurely, as if we had the whole night in front of us.

And we talked.

Actually, Claire did most of the talking. She spoke of her art and how much she liked to draw. She talked of her old neighborhood, her absent mother, and of her hopes and dreams and aspirations. Every so often, she'd look at me and ask a question about my life. As soon as I answered, she'd nod, toss out a pithy comment, and go right back to talking. I loved every soggy square of sidewalk that night.

As we passed Luigi's Italian restaurant, "Moon River" was playing. We stopped and looked through the big picture window; some ancient crooner with a silver toupee was belting his all into the microphone. It was the last song of the night, and he was singing to a half-dozen lingering customers. He had a nice voice that carried out into the street.

"Now I'll dance with you," I said.

Claire looked at me and smiled. She perched her party shoes on the windowsill, untied her toffee-brown hair, and let it fall down around her bare shoulders. She gave me her hands, and there we were, on a grimy sidewalk in the spring rain, dancing our first dance to "Moon River." Your mother later told me that was the moment she fell in love. After our impromptu dance, we held hands all the way home. From then on, we were never apart. Not one day. Not for the rest of her sweet life.

◆　◆　◆

When Pops finished his romantic tale, I waited for him to somehow tie it to my own situation, but he just took a bite of toast.

"Think we're too young?" I said.

He shrugged. "I'd be a hypocrite if I thought that. I was nineteen when I married your mother. She was eighteen."

"So . . . what then?" I said. "Cause I can tell when you've got something you want to say."

"Just be sure there are no regrets," Pops said. "Regrets can choke the life out of a marriage like nothing else." Then he winked at me. "That and leaving the toilet seat up."

CHAPTER SIX

Rebecca and I made a pact to keep our engagement secret until we could come up with a marriage plan. After all, we were both minors, and we didn't want the Waverlys panicking and doing something drastic—like packing up their only daughter and moving her to Switzerland.

Not long after I popped the question, Rebecca won the role of Juliet in her school's all-girl winter production of *Romeo and Juliet*. I managed to sneak in the back on opening night—keeping out of sight of her parents—and watched her light up the stage. Becca was magnetic as the young star-crossed lover. And as she uttered Juliet's immortal line *Good night, good night! Parting is such sweet sorrow,* her eyes found me lingering by the back door.

I proposed New Year's Eve at the center of the Wollman Rink, Central Park. It was cold, there was a crowd, and Rebecca—improbably and incredibly—said yes.

We were able to keep our secret hidden for all of three weeks. Then the Waverlys' housekeeper found the cubic zirconia ring I'd picked up for $19.99 at Kmart hidden between Becca's mattresses and took it to Mrs. Waverly. Mother confronted daughter, and the truth came tumbling out.

The reaction was predictably apoplectic. Jane Waverly blew up.

"Rebecca Anne, you will not see that boy again. Ever."

Rebecca later told me that her mother actually shed tears and told her that her beloved daughter had "let her down." They held a family meeting where, Rebecca said, it was obvious her mother had primed and prepped her father with the antiengagement talking points. She could tell that her dad was a reluctant participant in the discussion. While he no doubt agreed with his wife to a large degree, he was also one to let things run their course. He was smart enough to know that parental disapproval might well push us closer together. One evening, shortly after her parents had thrown down the gauntlet, Rebecca overheard her mother and father whispering in the study. Jack advised his high-strung wife that if she'd just relax, "the silly thing would fall on its own sword."

But Jane Waverly wasn't about to take that chance. She threw everything she had at her strong-willed daughter. At one point, she even threatened to disown her. Rebecca called her mother's bluff. "Disown away," she said. "I don't care. We'll elope and be done with it—and with you."

Of course, Jack Waverly's instincts were right. All of the opposition on the Waverlys' side only drove us closer together. "I know this must be right," Rebecca said. "Or my parents wouldn't oppose it so vigorously." Even though what Rebecca said made no sense, somehow it also felt right.

Frustrated that they couldn't simply command us to cease and desist, the Waverlys moved on to the next tack. Jack arranged to meet my dad at Tom's Diner in Brooklyn.

"I'd like to have a man-to-man," Jack told Hank on the phone.

Pops said he could tell from the moment he saw him that Rebecca's dad didn't want to be there. He hemmed and hawed for a good twenty minutes—anything to avoid the point—talking about sports and the weather and asking my dad about what it was like to drive a taxi. Pops later told me he liked Jack Waverly. "And, to be honest, I felt a little sorry for him."

Finally, Mr. Waverly got down to business. "I think our kids are making a very foolish decision. I think this marriage doesn't stand a chance, and they're only going to get hurt."

Pops agreed with him that we might be too young and that the decision to marry seemed impulsive and might well be a mistake. But then (as he told me later), my father explained to Jack Waverly why trying to tear us apart was a monumental exercise in futility.

"Jack, no matter what we do, love's going to find a way. You can throw up all sorts of barriers and roadblocks, but those kids are going to find a way around them. And all this scheming is only going to make them more determined."

He said Jack lowered his head and started peeling apart his paper napkin. "Tell me, Henry," he said at last. "Do you think those kids really and truly love each other?"

Pops shrugged. "Not for us to say what's in their hearts. But I'm willing to trust that they know what they're doing. Love's like water rushing down a river, Jack. Boulders and rocks might change its course, but it's still going down river."

Jack and Jane Waverly's campaign to derail our teenage wedding seemed to be dead on arrival. Pops was right. All their schemes and threats only made Rebecca and me more determined to see it through to the altar.

Then, one day, the mail arrived at the Waverly manse, and suddenly Mr. and Mrs. W's antiwedding campaign had new life.

◆ ◆ ◆

"Paul, I got into Yale."

It was on a crisp March Saturday morning at Bethesda Fountain that Rebecca uttered those fateful words. I knew right away we were in trouble. It was Yale. We'd hadn't really spoken about college, though it was always lingering somewhere in the back of my mind, and I knew it had to be in Rebecca's. My college options were limited. First of all, my grades were mediocre at best. I wasn't really a joiner, so I didn't have clubs and extracurricular activities to pad my résumé. My father had married and gone right to work after he graduated from high school, as had my mother, so advanced education wasn't in our family tree. Things were different for Rebecca Waverly.

Her parents had met at Yale the first week of freshman year. They had stayed heavily involved with their alma mater in the years since graduation, serving on various boards and alumni committees. From almost the moment of Rebecca's conception, they'd determined that their precious daughter would follow in their Ivy League footsteps. I knew that Yale had been a dream of Rebecca's as well, but not because her parents were Yalies. She was a fan of writer and Yale alumnus Thornton Wilder, who'd written her favorite play, *Our Town*.

"Paul, this doesn't affect us," she said. "You're the most important thing in my life. No matter what—our plans stay the same."

For some stupid reason, I believed her, even though the guilt that lingered continued to flare its nostrils. What if she woke up one morning and realized that I was a weight dragging her down?

"Becca, that's wonderful! Congratulations!" My words were sincere, my enthusiasm unfeigned, though I knew in my heart that this could well mean the end of the Paul-and-Rebecca story. But that was a worry for another time. I was proud of her. She'd gotten into Yale!

Rebecca threw her arms around me and kissed my lips. "I'm so relieved! I can't believe I thought you wouldn't be happy for me."

"Of course, I'm happy for you. You deserve this."

"We'll make things work, won't we?" Rebecca said. "We have to make things work."

"We will," I said. "Love will find a way."

That night at the dinner table, it took me a full ten minutes to eat one salmon patty, which I pushed around my plate like a hockey puck.

"You okay, son?" Pops asked.

I wasn't anywhere near okay. I really didn't believe love was going to find a way; I didn't see how it could. Rebecca couldn't turn down Yale, and even if she wanted to, I knew I couldn't let her. Yale was going to do what her parents had tried and failed to accomplish—drive a stake into the heart of our romance. Yale would mean opportunities for her, and new friends, and lots of young men from better families and with far better prospects than mine. *No,* I thought grimly. *We'll never survive Yale. Never.* I looked at my dad.

"Rebecca got into Yale."

Pops took a sip of iced tea and leaned forward. He got right to the point. "You think you're going to lose her?"

"Yeah. I know I'm going to lose her."

My dad crossed his hands the way he always did when he was about to impart some pearl of fatherly wisdom, folding his fingers together as if about to say grace.

"Son, love never comes easy. It often comes saddled with challenges and setbacks and impossible dilemmas. Love makes us struggle and fight and decide . . . decide if we want it enough to take on the struggle. Do you, son? Do you love Rebecca enough?"

"Pops, yes, but Yale is huge. It's a big accomplishment, and I don't want to get in her way."

"What are you afraid of, son? Really?"

I sighed and stabbed my plate with the fork I was gripping viselike in my right hand. "I'm afraid . . . I'm afraid that . . ." For a moment I wasn't sure if I wanted to say it, wasn't sure if I could vocalize my deepest fear. Then I looked in my father's patient eyes, and it tumbled out. "I don't want to be her regret."

Pops digested my words for a moment and then nodded slowly, as if he'd known all along what I'd been hiding. He leaned in, about to share some deep, dark secret.

"Son, I know. Yale is a big thing, and you're right, it may make things harder for you two—at least for a while. But . . . you wanna know something? I think you're worth it. And if you think Rebecca's gonna go off to college and find somebody better than you, then I'd advise you to think again. Cause you're no chopped liver. And I know that girl's got a good head on her shoulders—not because she got into Yale, but because she chose you. Now, I know you think Yale's this amazing opportunity, and it is. But don't go selling yourself short. Because . . . buddy . . . if you wanna know the truth . . . Yale doesn't hold a candle to you."

Despite Pops' encouraging words, I lay in bed that night staring at the ceiling and agonizing over what Becca's big news would mean for us. She had to go. It was the Ivy League, a dream come true. I chastised myself for moving so quickly. I never should have proposed that soon. We'd have to put our plans on hold for a while. I figured I could get a job or take a few courses at Borough of Manhattan Community College—maybe even work toward a degree. We'd have to pivot and improvise.

Who was I kidding? If I stayed in New York and Rebecca went to Yale, the Vegas odds didn't look good for our romantic longevity. I imagined her over in her bedroom at that very moment, staring at her own ceiling, trying to figure out a way to let me down easy. I suddenly hated that summer camp, hated that storm and the little stranded girl in the canoe. I hated how I felt and the pain of the heartbreak . . . I knew was coming.

CHAPTER SEVEN

I awoke the next morning to the phone ringing. After three rings, I figured Pops had gone out for his Sunday morning bagel and coffee, so I picked up.

"Hello?"

"May I please speak with Paul?"

I immediately recognized the deep baritone. Becca's father.

"This is Paul," I said.

"Hello, Paul. Jack Waverly."

My mind skipped around frantically. Why was Jack Waverly calling me on a Sunday morning? Had I done something wrong? Was Rebecca okay?

"Mrs. Waverly and I would like to invite you over for brunch. If you're available."

I was silent a moment too long.

"Hello?" Jack said.

"Oh," I said. "When?"

"How about now? My driver's waiting for you outside."

I slipped out of bed, shuffled to the window and looked down. Sure enough, a black Lincoln Town Car was idling in the street. What was going on?

"Could I speak to Becca, please?" I said. I thought she could clue me in.

"Rebecca's not at home this morning," Jack said. "We'd prefer she not know about this."

I again responded with stony silence.

"There's nothing to worry about," Becca's father said. I could hear the phony reassuring smile in his voice. I felt a little like a doomed mafioso in *The Godfather*, going on that last car ride everybody knew he wasn't coming back from. "Mrs. Waverly and I would just like to get to know you a little better."

◆ ◆ ◆

As I walked into the polished, perfect foyer of the Waverlys' luxurious Carnegie Hill apartment, I felt like I was there to be fitted for my own custom-made pair of cement shoes.

"Paul, thank you so much for coming on such short notice," Jane Waverly said. She clasped my hands and gave me a kiss on the cheek. I felt my stomach tighten. Michael Corleone kissed his brother Fredo, too, and we all know how that worked out.

Jack grasped my hand warmly. "Hope you brought your appetite."

What's going on here? I thought. I pictured my dad finding the hasty note I'd left under a magnet on the refrigerator:

Brunch with Becca's parents. See you later.

Would he think that they had lured me into some kind of trap? I wished I'd seen him before I'd left. He could have thrown me some parting advice or, even better, forbidden me from going altogether. I strategized. Maybe I should front them out—tell them that I knew the reason for the spur-of-the-moment invitation and was wise to their scheming ways. But the truth was I had no idea why they wanted to see me. Maybe it was a harmless social call. Maybe they really did want to get to know me better.

Who was I kidding?

"Thanks for having me," I said.

"The pleasure is all ours," Jane said. Mom and daughter had the same smile. She took my coat and scarf, gave them to her husband to hang up, and then put her hand on my arm. "Come. Brunch is served."

As Mrs. Waverly escorted me to the dining room, I wondered what they had done with Rebecca. What story had they fed her to get her out of the apartment so they could enact their clandestine plot?

"So, where's Rebecca?" I asked as we stepped into the dining room.

Jane let go of my arm and smiled. "She's out with her auntie. They're spending the morning together."

Good one, I thought. *Now you're free to work me over without your meddling daughter's interference.*

A part of me wondered if Rebecca was in on it. What if my worst fears had been correct, and she was complicit in the strange and sudden brunch? Maybe she'd decided to end things with me and had tasked her parents with the dirty work. That didn't seem like Rebecca, at least not the Rebecca who'd plunged into the stormy lake without so much as a flicker of hesitation. I looked at the breakfast spread laid out on the perfect table. Over eggs Benedict, Canadian bacon, and French toast, I would soon learn the devious truth.

I'd only managed a sip of fresh-squeezed grapefruit juice when the Waverlys made their feelings clear. With a glance at her husband, Mother Jane took the lead.

"Paul, you know Rebecca thinks the world of you. And Jack and I think you're a fine young man." I looked at Jack, and he pretended to study the stem of his monogrammed sterling silver fork. His refusal to meet my eye was an ominous sign.

Jane continued. "Now, I know that may be difficult to believe, considering we've expressed some . . . opposition to your . . . engagement." The E word caught in her throat. I looked back at Jack. He continued his flatware fixation. I thought how the whole affair felt rehearsed, and I was almost certain they'd done a run-through before I'd arrived. "But it was never personal," Jane said. "We just didn't . . . don't believe Rebecca is ready for such a commitment."

Jane looked at Jack as if waiting for him to chime in. When he remained silent, she shot him a hard glare and continued. "And . . . as you are no doubt aware . . . Rebecca has been admitted to Yale for the fall." Jane Waverly spoke with the practiced diction of a 1940s B-movie actress.

"Yes," I said. "I'm happy for her. She deserves it." And I sounded like some politician regurgitating the party line.

"Aren't you sweet," Jane said. "Did you hear that, Jack?"

"I heard it," Jack said. His tone was clipped. He still couldn't meet my eye. I thought she might be kicking him under the table.

"So magnanimous," Jane said. "Considering how it's going to impact your . . . relationship." *Relationship.* Another word that seemed to stick in her gullet.

Oh boy, I thought. *Here it comes. The buried lede has been exhumed.* I dabbed my mouth with a linen napkin and looked her in the eye. I thought feigning confusion was my best play.

"What do you mean?" I asked. It was the obvious question, but I wasn't an idiot; I knew where this ship was headed. Jane Waverly was practically gleeful with the knowledge that venerable old Yale would put a fork in our young and impetuous love. And as I looked in her steel-blue eyes, I knew that it wasn't just marriage this woman wanted to derail. She wanted to make sure I was exiled from her daughter's life ad infinitum. She wanted to make sure Paul Bennett was not even a footnote on the Waverly family tree.

Jane chuckled as if my question seemed silly. "Well," she said, "you won't be able to spend time together anymore. However, I seriously doubt a handsome and well-bred young man like you will be on the market long. Some lucky young lady will snatch you right up."

"Maybe," I said. "Then again . . . I guess Becca could decide . . ." I let my unfinished thought hang in the air, took my time, had a bite of bacon, a sip of juice. ". . . not to go to Yale . . . at all."

I knew that would sting, wanted it to sting, and I was right. I'd found my mark. Up until my private brunch with Mother and Father Waverly, I'd assumed Rebecca and Yale were a done deal. But there at the Waverly breakfast table, I could see that my impertinent words had pricked off a scab of obvious contention. Could it be Rebecca Waverly was . . . wavering? Why else would they invite me to brunch if Yale was a fait accompli? Why would they need to speak to me at all?

I felt the mood shift instantly, the gratuitous sheen in Jane's eyes turning on a dime. She was done playing nice with the poor boy from Brooklyn.

"Oh, she's going," Jane said. "Jack and I met at Yale. We're both members of the Board of Governors. It has been our desire . . . our expectation . . . that our only daughter continue the legacy. We know Rebecca wants the same thing . . ."

I'm right! Rebecca isn't sure about Yale. I felt a surge of confidence. It was me. *I* was the reason she wasn't sure. Paul T. Bennett.

"However," Jane went on, "lately, for some inexplicable reason, Rebecca Anne's been vacillating in her resolve. And that has Jack and me concerned. Right, dear?"

"Sure," Jack said. "Concerned."

Jane dabbed her lips with a napkin and smiled at me. "We need your help, Paul. You strike us as a reasonable young man, and we know you want what's best for Rebecca. You do, right?"

There was an awkward silence, and I could feel them waiting for me to fill it. I decided to keep them hanging.

"You do want what's best for Rebecca . . . don't you?" Jane spoke as if she assumed I simply didn't hear her the first time.

I felt my cheeks flush, annoyed at her condescending tone. I resented the fact she'd lobbed me a question that had but one reasonable response. But I also felt a strange sense of euphoria. For once, the son of a cab driver had the power.

"Of course I do," I said. "But maybe we should let Rebecca decide what is and what isn't *best* for her. Maybe Yale is best . . . maybe not. Maybe marrying me and living in a double-wide is best for her. Nobody really knows."

I caught a glance from Jack, and though I couldn't be completely sure, I thought I detected a flicker of admiration in his gray eyes. Jane's eyes showed me nothing but disdain. It seemed she hadn't prepared for resistance from some Brooklyn upstart. And she certainly didn't seem to find any humor in my snarky double-wide comment.

"Let us be clear," she said. I could almost see her yanking off the gloves. She glared at Jack. Apparently, he'd been tasked with delivering the kill shot.

"We want you out of the picture," he said. Despite the bluntness of his assertion, I could tell the words pained him, as if I were a wounded bunny writhing on his lawn that he could no longer bear to watch suffer. I felt the blood run to the tips of my ears.

Jane tried to soften his blow. "The college years are the best years of one's life. Rebecca deserves to enjoy the experience to the fullest without any . . ." She struggled to find the right words. I helped her out.

"Dead weight," I said.

Jane and Jack exchanged a look. I'd nailed it. I could see a glimmer of hope in their faces. *Maybe the boy's finally getting it.*

I folded my napkin and pushed back from the mahogany dining table. "Thank you for breakfast." I got up and started for the door. I needed to find Rebecca and fast. I needed to see her face and watch her react with outrage at her parents' dastardly brunch attack. I threw on my coat and turned to find that Jane and Jack had followed me to the foyer.

When Jane spoke there were tears in her eyes. She was going for the jugular. "I know you must think we're snobbish and elitist."

"Yes," I said. "I know you are." I was weary of playing the deferential guest.

Jane nodded. "Fair enough. But try to understand. Rebecca's our only daughter. Our only child. She's not yet eighteen years old. And she deserves a chance to be great. She deserves a chance to experience life, to explore all her options before she makes a choice that will no doubt end her youth and ruin her opportunity to see what she can truly be. And—whether you believe it or not—the same goes for you. I know Rebecca thinks she's in love, but Paul, if she chooses you over Yale, it will be a stupid, impulsive decision she'll end up regretting for the rest of her life. I know that sounds cold and harsh, but I believe in my heart it's the truth. And if you would put aside your own self-interests, even for a moment, I believe you'd come to the same conclusion. Ask yourself, Paul. Would you rather be Rebecca's first great love, or her greatest regret?"

I didn't say goodbye, allowing my feet to carry me numbly to the curb. The town car was not waiting to take me back to the wrong side of the tracks. As I hoofed it the four blocks to the Ninety-Fourth Street subway station, an unexpected feeling welled inside me, rising up from the pit of my stomach to my chest and into my throat. I knew then so clearly what I should have known all along.

I didn't deserve Rebecca Waverly.

CHAPTER EIGHT

Dear Rebecca . . .

My first instinct was to find Rebecca as soon as I could and confront her. I was going to call her out, force her to make a choice right then and there. On the spot.

"Me or Yale. You choose."

Of course, Becca would protest. She'd try to reassure me that her going to Yale didn't have to adversely affect our relationship, that she wouldn't let it. She'd counter her mother's arguments, promise that our love would win out. I'd want to believe her, but deep down, I'd hear Jane Waverly's words echoing in my head. Try as I might to silence them, I knew I wouldn't be able to. I could never compete with Yale. Rebecca would make new friends, wealthy and smart people like her. She'd meet young men with brilliant futures and summer homes on Martha's Vineyard. They'd eventually want to know about whom she was dating, and she'd have to tell them about me—the cab driver's son from Brooklyn working a double shift at some record store or pizza joint just to afford train fare to come see her on the weekends. She'd tell me it didn't matter, that she loved me no matter what, and she might even believe it at first. Over time we'd drift, and Rebecca would wake up one day and realize she'd changed, that the gulf between our disparate worlds was simply too wide to bridge.

By the time I bounded up the steps to Prospect Park, I'd decided that face-to-face was not the way to go. I would call her, have it out on the phone. As I reached my own home stoop, I'd switched gears again. I was going to write her a letter. After all, I was a writer, and that was my strong suit. I wouldn't tell her about my clandestine brunch with her parents. I'd simply lay out the cold, hard facts. I was doing her a favor. If she took the out I was offering, then her parents were right. In her heart of hearts, Rebecca really did yearn for Yale and the life that came with it.

My hand trembled as I gripped the ballpoint pen. This letter could very well end the best thing that had ever happened to me. My first drafts were long and rambling and overly sentimental. Finally, I settled on curt simplicity.

> *Dear Rebecca,*
> *This is the hardest letter I've ever had to write. I know that Yale is a wonderful opportunity for you, and I think it's best that you take that opportunity free of any obligations. The last thing I want to do is hold you back and keep you from fulfilling your potential. With that in mind, I bid you farewell. I think we should go our separate ways. I wish you all the best now and in the future. I won't forget you.*
> *Fondly,*
> *Paul T. Bennett*

It was formal and businesslike and sounded like something out of a Jane Austen novel. As I walked down to the mailbox on the corner, I tried to imagine her opening it. What would her reaction be? Sadness? Shock? Relief? I hoped for the first two, but the sinking feeling in my stomach told me it would probably be the latter. I poised my hand over the slot.

I knew once I let go of that little envelope, the die would be cast. There would be no going back. I took a deep breath and dropped the letter in.

I spent the next three days holed up in my attic room, coming out only to go to the bathroom and retrieve the tray of food Pops left outside my door three times a day. He'd always tap on the door as he dropped it off, ask if I needed anything or wanted to talk. My response was always the same.

"Thanks. I'm good."

Time and again, I'd hear the phone ring. Time and again, Pops would call up to me.

"Son. Rebecca's on the phone."

"Tell her I'm asleep."

"Tell her I'm not here."

"Tell her I'm dead."

My heart wasn't just broken; it was obliterated. I imagined thousands of tiny heart pieces floating around in my chest cavity. Rebecca was my first girlfriend—therefore I had exactly zero experience with the intensity of heartbreak. Of course, I'd heard the tired old clichés such as *Everything happens for a reason*; *If you were meant to be together, you'd be together*; and the classic *There are other fish in the sea*. These worn-out lines offered me little solace as I sulked in my room. The radio was no help either—it was as if the deejay had heard the news of our breakup and was taunting me. This pathetic parade included "Unbreak My Heart," "Yesterday," and "I Will Always Love You."

Halfway through day two of my grieving, my dad slid a note beneath the door asking if I had any idea when I might emerge. He was concerned about me missing so much school. I scrawled a few words on the bottom of the note and shoved it back under the door.

No immediate plans. Check back in a week. See if I'm still alive.

Near the end of the third day, there was a light tap on the door, and my dad's quiet voice called through the crack.

"Buddy? Can I come in?" Though nearing my stir-crazy tipping point and eager for human contact, I was torn. But then he uttered three words that snapped the fraying strings of my resolve. "I have pie."

The pie was peach, a dessert I simply hadn't the will power to resist no matter how badly my heart was broken. It was warm, and Pops had plopped on a scoop of vanilla ice cream that had mostly melted, giving the pie a creamy white coating. Just the way I liked it.

As I sat on the edge of my unkempt bed enjoying the tasty bribe, Pops pulled up a chair across from me. I braced for "the talk," waited for him to pepper me with reasonableness. I figured he might even spout a few breakup clichés I hadn't heard. Something like *There's a cover for every pot* or *When one door closes, another one opens*. I knew he'd be wasting his time. I'd lost Rebecca. All the fatherly wisdom in the world couldn't cure that ill or make the pain go away.

"Is it hopeless?" Pops said. I looked at him. The question threw me. I wasn't sure what he meant. He sensed my confusion. "The situation with your girl . . . is it hopeless?" I nodded.

"Totally. Irretrievably."

"Good," he said. I looked up from my pie, and he smiled as if my answer had solved everything and life could go back to normal.

"Good?"

"It's good," Pops said, "because then you'll stop worrying about it. If there's no hope, you won't waste your energy. You'll accept that there's absolutely nothing you can do. What's done is done."

"I still don't get why that's a good thing," I said.

"Ever hear the phrase *Let go and let God*?"

"Too many times," I said. "It's become cliché."

Pops chuckled. "Usually a cliché's cliché because it's true. The thing is . . . what most people don't get . . . when you let go, you can't do it partway. You've got to pry off every finger. Surrender. Raise the white flag. Throw in the towel. Give up all preconceived notions as to how things might work out. And that's when God moves in. *Not my will, but thine, be done. Not my will, but thine.*"

Pops reached out, tousled my hair, and stood up. His talks were always short and to the point, and once he'd had his say, he beat a hasty retreat so I could start thinking things over. "All's gonna work out," he said. "You just wait and see."

His words were wise and comforting and perfect. And I would like to say that I believed him, that the moment he walked out of the room I could hear the *Rocky* theme playing in my head. Didn't work out that way. I went to bed that night just as hopeless as before, just as certain my life was over. Then, a little bit after midnight, there was a plunk on my bedroom window. I sat up with a start and threw off the blanket.

I flicked on the bedside lamp, went over to the window, and saw that the pane was cracked. A tiny fissure spread out glass spider legs. At first, I thought it was one of the idiot Parker brothers who lived a few doors down. They pretty much ran the show at their house, had no curfew or rules, and had thrown rocks at our house before. I'd later learned it was a pebble that had done the damage, a tiny rock meant for the shutters.

I could barely make out a shape when I peered down from my attic room onto our dark postage-stamp lawn. The streetlights in front of our house had been burned out for months, and the one opposite us only faintly illuminated the shape standing in our yard. But when the shape spoke, I knew the voice instantly.

"Paul, it's me."

Rebecca stepped into a dim, narrow shaft of light. She was in jeans and T-shirt, her ruby hair tied back in a ponytail—just like the first time I saw her at the edge of the lake.

"Becca, what are you doing here?" I was stunned to see her, thrilled to see her. I tried to imagine why in the world she was in our yard in the middle of the night, and how she'd managed to escape her overly protective parents.

"I have to talk to you," she said. "I'm going to climb up."

As I tried to envision how she'd accomplish that task, my dad's voice carried out from a downstairs window.

"No need for that. Front door's unlocked."

A minute later a miracle had happened—Becca, the love of my life, was sitting on the edge of my bed. I straddled my desk chair and watched her intently, waiting. She pulled my old ratty maroon woolen scarf from her back pocket and tossed it at me. "I found this on a hook by our front door. My parents failed to get rid of the evidence."

I felt like a suspect in the police interrogation room confronted with the smoking gun.

"I know why you were there," she said. "I made my parents confess their stupid plan. To be honest, I wasn't all that surprised they'd use Yale to try to split us up. What I can't figure out though is why you'd go along with it. I thought you were smarter than that."

I looked down at the scarf in my hand. I was ashamed. She had me. There wasn't much I could say.

"You hurt me," Becca said. Her tone was level. She wasn't trying to make me feel bad and wasn't looking for an explanation. She was simply stating a fact.

"Rebecca, I'm . . ."

"Shhh. I'm not done." She glared at me to let me know she was serious. "Paul, I know your intentions were honorable, and that you were doing what was best for me. But I don't need you to rescue me. And I sure don't need you to decide my future. I get to choose what's best for me. I get to choose my life." She shook her head at me as if I were a little brat caught with his hand in the cookie jar.

"Becca, I'm . . ."

"Shush! Still not finished. You are so lucky, Paul Bennett. You are so lucky that I'm willing to give you another chance." She pinched her forefinger and thumb in the air. "You came this close to blowing it. Lucky for you . . . I've decided to forgive you. Don't make me regret it."

"But, Becca . . . I don't know how it's going to work. I mean, I guess I could move with you and get a job somewhere. I'm not even sure where Yale is . . ." Becca tossed a pillow at me.

"New Haven, Connecticut. But that's irrelevant."

"Why is it irrelevant?" I said.

Rebecca shook her head. "Boy, you are so dense. Don't you get it? I'm not going to Yale. I've turned them down."

I stared at her. Was she serious? "Becca, are you sure . . . ?"

"Paul, will you stop it! I know what I want, and I've made my decision. I know it's the right one. And it's not because I think Yale would be the end of our relationship. That's silly."

"But Yale is your dream," I said.

Becca looked at me and shook her head as if she couldn't believe someone could be so dense. "Yale's not my dream, Paul. You are." She let her words sink in and then crossed her arms. "Now, I'd like you to apologize." I tried to smile, but her look shut me down. She had me dead to rights.

"I . . . apologize."

"For what?" she said.

"For . . . being such a . . . jerk."

"And . . . ?" she said. I looked in her eyes. I wasn't sure what she meant. She mouthed "the letter."

"And . . . for that . . . letter. That lame letter."

She burned me with her hazel eyes, and I could tell she wasn't quite satisfied. My eyes welled up as it slowly dawned on me that I had lost her and, by some miracle, been given a reprieve. I'd blown it, and God had given me a second chance.

"Rebecca, I'm so, so sorry I hurt you. I didn't mean it, but I wanted you to . . . I want you to be happy. I want you to have a good life. A life without regrets."

Rebecca motioned me over, and I sat beside her on the bed. She took my hand and patted it like my mother used to.

"We will have a good life, Paul Bennett. A wonderful life. We'll make it together. I don't know what the future holds . . . but I know I want to spend mine with you. Now, stop trying to play hero, and kiss me."

CHAPTER NINE

"As we, the girls of Brearley, move out into the world, my hope is that we will do so with the courage and trust that God moves before us, guiding and guarding our every step along the often rugged, sometimes frightening . . . glorious path of life."

Despite a mild protest from my dad, I skipped my own hot, sweaty, and overcrowded high school graduation that toasty June 7 to hear Rebecca deliver her class salutatorian speech. She was fearless and dynamic, and I was beyond proud of her. I didn't even care that her parents didn't bother to save me a seat. With or without the approval of Jack and Jane Waverly, their only daughter was mine. We were married two weeks later.

Though Jack and Jane Waverly would never fully accept that their flawlessly brilliant daughter was skipping Yale to marry a cab driver's son, they finally realized they had no choice but to lay down their swords and grudgingly join the wedding planning. Rebecca made it clear that if they wanted a relationship with her going forward, they had to accept her decision. I'm sure the idea of never seeing their future grandchildren weighed on their elitist minds, so they ran up the white flag. The war was over.

Rebecca and I decided on a simple country wedding in a quaint white chapel a few miles from the summer camp where we first met.

We invited only a few dozen guests, who gobbled up most of the one- and two-star motel rooms that ran along New York State Route 42. We married on June 23, Rebecca's eighteenth birthday. There was standing room only in the tiny country chapel that humid Saturday afternoon. My dad put on a coat and tie for the first time since my mother's funeral, and I'd never seen him look happier.

And the church organist played "The Wedding March."

As I watched my Rebecca glide gracefully down the center aisle toward the altar, my thoughts again tiptoed over our short and eventful history. For a moment, I saw that awkward teenage girl again, standing in the storm, the rain soaking her red ponytail and streaming wet streaks down her freckled face. *What if it hadn't rained that day?* I thought. *What if the wind had blown in a different direction and pushed the storm a few miles south?* I knew in that moment that God had brought us that thunderstorm. He had sheltered that little lone camper out on the lake, keeping her safe from harm until we could rescue her. It wasn't chance, wasn't fate . . . it was all part of a plan, a perfect plan that had dodged bullets and brunches and all attempts to derail it. And there we were, against all odds, standing in that tiny church right where we belonged, right where God had put us. *We are destined to be together,* I thought. *And nothing will ever be able to tear us apart.*

As Rebecca reached the altar, she smiled and kissed her father on the cheek. Jack Waverly nodded to me and moved to take his seat in the front pew next to his wife and my dad. I held out my hand. Rebecca took it in hers, and I helped her step up onto the altar beside me.

Our pastor was the Reverend Russell Holloway, a towering African American third-generation preacher. He'd lost his left eye in Vietnam and wore a black pirate patch. He opened the ceremony with a joke I'm sure he'd made at many of the countless weddings he'd presided over.

"Ahoy, me hearties!" Even Jane Waverly, who looked like a woman having a root canal for most of the ceremony, cracked a smile at that one.

"I'd like to welcome all you city folks who've managed to find your way out to our little chapel on this sultry June afternoon," Reverend Holloway said. "Let me apologize that our air conditioning isn't working as well as either you or I hoped it would be. But I promise you that I'll keep it short. No more than two hours."

A nervous chuckle rolled through the congregation.

"Now, whenever I agree to perform a wedding ceremony, I like to sit down with family and friends of the bride and groom and find out a few things about them. It helps me know the couple a little better. And I have to tell you, Rebecca and Paul are two extraordinary young people. First, let's start with Rebecca."

My bride and I exchanged a look. What in the world was he going to say?

"Let me take you way back in time to when Rebecca was a mere sixteen years old." The minister grinned. "I guess that wasn't so long ago, was it?" The congregation chuckled, and Rebecca blushed. "She was sixteen and the world's biggest Yo-Yo Ma fan. Now, if you don't know Yo-Yo, let me tell you, he's a cellist. A very famous cellist." Rebecca smiled at me. She knew where the story was going.

"Well, imagine how thrilled she was when her best friend, Cara, came up to her at school and handed her an envelope."

Maid of honor Cara raised her hand. "That's me."

Another peal of laughter rolled through the wooden benches. The pastor seemed to be thoroughly enjoying himself. He continued. "'Happy early birthday,' Cara here said to Rebecca. Rebecca peeled open that envelope. And there they were: two tickets to Yo-Yo Ma at Carnegie Hall. Opening night. Eighth row center. Well, Rebecca did what any sixteen-year-old Yo-Yo Ma fanatic would do: she squealed and jumped up and down." Another rippling chuckle echoed through the sanctuary. I could see our wedding guests using all manner of pamphlets and church literature to fan themselves, but they sure weren't bored.

The reverend continued. "Now, there was a cleaning lady who worked for the Waverlys named Rosa. She'd been working for them for a number of years, and sometimes she would bring her son Rico to work with her. Rico was about Rebecca's age, and they would play together when they were little. Some might say that Rico was a little slow, what you might call developmentally disabled. Not long after Rebecca received the gift of Yo-Yo Ma, Rico was at the house with his mother and, like always, gave Rebecca a big hug the moment he saw her. Then he just blurted it out. 'Rebecca, will you go to my prom with me?'"

I looked at Rebecca. I could see her eyes welling up, and she was struggling to keep from streaking her mascara. I took her hands as the reverend continued.

"Without even asking any questions, Rebecca said, 'Sure, Rico. Of course I'll go with you. Thanks for asking.' It was only later she found out that Rico's prom was on the same night as Yo-Yo. When Rosa found this out, she told Rebecca not to worry about it—said that she'd break the news to her son. Rebecca looked her right in the eye and said, 'What news?'

"'The news that you won't be able to go to Rico's dance with him,' Rosa said.

"'Oh, I'm going to his prom,' Rebecca said. 'Besides, I've already picked out my dress.'" I felt Rebecca's grip on my hands tighten as her tears broke free and streamed down her cheeks. Her wedding makeup was ruined, and we hadn't even begun our vows.

Reverend Holloway wasn't finished. "Now, I'm sad to say that young Rico passed away this past fall. And when I called his mother to ask her about this story, she told me that his most prized possession was the boutonniere that Rebecca gave him the night of his prom. She said he kept it in a little glass filled with water on his dresser. Long after that flower had shriveled up and died, he kept it there in water as if hoping that one day it was going to bloom all over again."

I glanced out at the audience. There wasn't a dry eye in the sanctuary. Then the reverend moved on to me. Fortunately for the melting audience, my story was short and nowhere near as compelling or heroic as my bride's. He told of an Easter egg hunt at a neighborhood rec center when I was seven years old. The teenage volunteers had hidden, among the dozens of ordinary candy eggs, a giant chocolate egg wrapped in gold foil. They announced that the finder of the "golden egg" would be awarded a large Easter basket chock full of jellybeans, and marshmallow Peeps and Cadbury Crème Eggs. And—most importantly—a big hollow chocolate bunny.

"Paul here was at least two years older than the next oldest egg hunter," the pastor said, "and totally obsessed with procuring that golden egg. He was determined to own that basket. So when the whistle blew, he let less experienced egg hunters have the low hanging fruit—the eggs hidden in plain sight—while our future groom here focused on the big prize. It took him all of thirty seconds to figure out that, as there was only one tree on the whole lot, it was probably hidden somewhere in that tree. Lo and behold, he found the golden prize tucked beneath, covered by leaves. Young Paul jumped up and called out in triumph. 'I've got it! I've found the golden egg!'"

Rebecca snickered, and I shrugged. The reverend continued, milking as much drama as he could out of my lackluster Easter story. "As they were presenting him his Easter prize, young Paul noticed a little girl with blond pigtails standing in back of the crowd. She was maybe three years old and had big tears rolling down her cheeks."

In actuality, I couldn't remember if she was really three or had pigtails, but I figured the good pastor was due some creative license. I do remember she was crying: wailing as if a fishing hook had lodged in her eyeball. Her mother was standing beside her, arm on her shoulders, comforting.

"And what did our Paul do at that moment?" Reverend Holloway asked. I winked at Rebecca, who was smiling at me. I wanted to confess to her that my first instinct was to grab that basket and run home. "I'll tell you what he did," the pastor said. "He walked right over and handed that basket to the little girl."

An audible swoon came from the women in the pews. I saw Rebecca doing her best to keep from bursting out laughing. I squeezed her hand.

"It was a gesture of unselfishness," the reverend said. "And it shows that Paul is a kind and giving person and, perhaps, even deserving of a bride as special as Rebecca Anne Waverly."

"I wouldn't go *that* far," Rebecca whispered.

With our stories out of the way, the good reverend finally moved on to the actual marrying part. He read Bible passages that were both appropriate and moving, finishing with a profound verse from Colossians.

"*And over all these virtues put on love, which binds them all together in perfect unity.*'"

Rebecca and I had decided it'd be fun to write our own wedding vows and, while doing so, to err on the side of humor over sappiness.

"I, Paul Thomas Bennett, do solemnly swear to put up with Rebecca Anne Waverly's weirdness and total lack of taste in music . . ."

"I, Rebecca Anne Waverly, do reluctantly agree to accept and endure Paul Thomas Bennett's many, many glaring faults, including, but not limited to, his truly horrific taste in clothes . . ."

As the best day of my life came to a close, and Becca and I headed off to begin our new adventure, I pondered the minister's final words to the bride and groom:

"Two are better than one, because they have a good return for their labor: if either of them falls down, one can help the other up."

I held her hand in the car all the way to the hotel, close to tears, although I never told Becca that. For the first time in my life, I was part of something bigger than myself, and I prayed that the indescribable joy I felt would never go away.

The day after our wedding, Rebecca and I bid farewell to our respective families and drove off in the old converted taxicab my dad had bought for us as a wedding present. The empty cans tied to the bumper clanked and clanged as we put our old lives in the rearview mirror. We were young, in love, and heady with our new freedom.

A month before our wedding, we'd still been kicking around possible places to begin our married life. I had suggested we head out to the Northwest—maybe find a place near Seattle. Rebecca had vetoed that on account of excessive rain and pushed for New Mexico, but I wasn't really a desert guy. We had gone round and round for weeks until Rebecca finally brought our debate to a conclusion with a simple statement.

"I'm going to pray about it."

A week after this declaration, Rebecca picked up a travel magazine in her dentist's waiting room and opened it to a spread on quaint small towns called "New England's Hidden Gems," page-flipping right to a photo of a town square in Manchester, Maine. Her prayers had been answered. The moment she saw the charming downtown with its brick storefronts, center green, gazebo, and tall white-spired church, she knew Manchester would be our home.

"It seems like a good place to put down roots," Rebecca said, showing me the magazine she'd swiped from her dentist. "Doesn't it seem perfect?" I flipped through the photo spread, and it seemed to me, well, small.

"Shouldn't we at least visit first?"

Rebecca took my hand. "We don't need to. I just have a feeling. Trust my feeling." She smiled and gave me a kiss on the cheek.

I took another look at the photo of the town square. "Okay," I said. "I'll trust your feeling."

So there we were, heading north, rolling along a country highway, singing along to a golden oldies radio station. I smiled at my beautiful new bride sitting in the passenger seat, wondering what I'd done to deserve such a gift. I was an ordinary bloke, as the British would say, yet somehow, I had this wife sitting across from me—a woman of such extraordinary grace and beauty that it seemed I was terribly miscast as her husband. I chuckled and shook my head.

"What?" Rebecca said. She put a hand on my arm.

"Nothing," I said. "I'm just thinking about our future."

"What are you doing that for? Enjoy the moment."

Just as she said that, a song came on the radio as if the deejay had gazed into my head and read my thoughts: "We May Never Pass This Way Again," by Seals and Crofts. Halfway through the second verse, Rebecca started to sing along, and I joined in.

> We may never pass this way again,
> that's why I want it with you.
> Cause you make me feel like I'm more than a friend.
> Like I'm the journey and you're the journey's end.
> We may never pass this way again.
> That's why I want it with you, baby.

Yes, life was good for Mr. and Mrs. Bennett, and the future was ours for the taking. But when we arrived in pristine Manchester and rolled through the town square on a perfect summer evening, I had one clear and immediate thought.

This is it?

It somehow looked larger in the magazine spread. Downtown was a collage of charming shops, stores, and cafes that framed a center green. There was an old Victorian bandstand like the one where Bill Murray danced with Andie MacDowell in *Groundhog Day*. It all seemed so ideal, so thoroughly American—only a little tinier than I was used to.

Rebecca seemed almost starstruck as we rolled through town for the first time. "It's like a Norman Rockwell painting," she said. "Or a Currier and Ives postcard. I bet they really do it up special at

Christmastime." It wasn't even summer yet, and my blushing bride was already envisioning a towering Christmas tree, bows and holly, and lights. While she gushed at pretty much everything she was seeing out the car window, I was more circumspect. And to be honest, I was having a hard time imagining starting a new life there. But as I looked over at Rebecca, the glow on her face told me she'd come home—for the very first time.

"Look at it, Paul. Isn't it wonderful?"

I smiled and did my best to muster enthusiasm. "Yeah. It's nice."

She took my hand, holding it the same way she had the night she'd first shown me the pictures in the magazine. "Just wait. You're going to love it here."

CHAPTER TEN

When we first arrived in Manchester, Rebecca and I used some of our wedding money to rent a tiny cottage on the outskirts of town. It was cozy, comfortable, and cheap. There was one bedroom and a little den with a fireplace. We loved the weathered redwood deck out back, with an unbalanced metallic table and two peeling deck chairs where we sat and ate dinner together on balmy evenings. The cottage had a narrow pine-needle-covered path behind it that meandered through the woods for a mile or so and ended up at Waller's Pond, a lovely little lake where locals went for picnics in spring and summer, took strolls in the fall, and ice-skated all winter. We took that walk almost every evening and would end up sitting on the old bench at the end of the dock, talking and planning and looking ahead. Almost always the talk worked its way around to our unborn children.

"So," Becca would say. "How many do you want?"

"Two's a nice number," I'd usually say. Sometimes I'd throw her off and modify my response to three. Even if I threw out seven or eight, she'd always agree with me and lean her head on my shoulder. I'd ease my arm around her, and we'd sit in silence, gazing out on the still pond. Those are the moments that made me want to click pause so that I could stay in that still frame a while longer. Judging from the sound of her contented sighs, Rebecca felt the same.

Our landlady had a daughter who was a Realtor, and a couple months after arriving in Manchester, we took the remainder of our wedding nest egg and made a down payment on a charming Victorian fixer-upper at 25 Bethlehem Place, a quiet tree-lined street four blocks from the town square Rebecca had fallen in love with that day in the dentist's office.

The house had a wraparound front porch that creaked in all the right places. The first floor included a parlor, kitchen, and den, and there was a master bedroom and three smaller rooms upstairs. One of them looked out on the backyard and to the woods beyond. Rebecca's face lit up the first moment she stood at the window and saw that view.

"Dibs," she said. "This room will be my art studio."

As Rebecca and I stood side by side gazing dreamily out the window of that second-floor room, the Realtor stepped up beside us.

"In the winter you can see all the way to Waller's Pond," she said.

Nestled at the rear of the property, about twenty yards from the back porch, was a tool shed I thought might make a good writer's shack, the cozy little space where I would pen my great American novel. So while Rebecca chatted with our agent, I pushed open the creaky door of the dilapidated shed and gave myself a tour of the dusty, cobwebbed hideaway. And there, perched on a rickety old table, was an ancient vintage Underwood typewriter. It was as if God were winking at me, letting me know my writer's space instincts were on the mark.

I leaned down and blew the dust off the keys. An old yellowed sheet of paper was tucked in the platen. I carefully pulled it out and shook off the dust. There was a single short phrase typed on the sheet that I recognized from 1 Corinthians, verse 13:

And now these three remain: faith, hope, and love. But the greatest of these is love.

We moved into our first home, at 25 Bethlehem Place, on our three-month wedding anniversary. The next day, I started work as a mail carrier for the Manchester Post Office.

"Just temporary," I said, standing in our open front door that morning. Rebecca straightened my shirt collar.

"I'm proud of you," she said. "And you're the cutest mailman I've ever seen."

We kissed goodbye, and I headed off for my first day on the job. I paused at the end of the front walk and turned back to see her watching me. "Till my novel's published," I said. She blew me a kiss.

"I don't care if all you ever become is a Manchester mail carrier," she said. "I'll love you anyway." I smiled, sent her a kiss back, and headed out the gate. I was going to be a great American novelist, and Rebecca dreamed of being the world's most famous landscape artist. I had my typewriter and paper; she had her paints and canvas. And so we started out, two dreamers in love.

I settled in fairly quickly to my mailman routine. My boss, Postmaster Ray Waldrop, was a little rough around the edges, but seemed to be a good guy. I trained with local legend "Mailman George," the eighty-one-year-old career postal employee who was retiring to Florida to live with his son and family. For an entire week, George took me door to door along his route and introduced me to his customers. He moved slowly, and I could tell that every step he took made him wince a little. He never mentioned it.

I was impressed by how much he knew about everybody along the route. He knew children's and grandchildren's names, their birthdates, what sports they played, and what they wanted to be when they grew up. George seemed more like the family doctor than the mail carrier.

"Been walking this route since 1958," George said. "I know every crack in the pavement, and more importantly, I know these people. And not just their names and addresses either. I know their lives. Most of them consider me a part of the family."

"You're going to be a hard act to follow," I said.

He looked at me. "You better believe it. But you sure better try. If I hear you're selling these fine folks short, I'm gonna come back up from Florida and give you a good thrashing." He smiled and gave me a wink to let me know he was only kidding. "They deserve the best of you," he said. "That's what I tried to give."

As we slowly worked our way through the quiet neighborhoods, I got to hear again and again how much the customers loved George, and how much they were going to miss him. Most were welcoming and kind when he introduced his young replacement, but some were a little aloof and weren't shy about speaking their mind right in front of me.

"Nobody can ever replace you, George."

"George, why don't you stay and send this kid to Florida?"

"Who'll talk politics with me when you're gone, George?"

George would always soak in the compliments and flattery and then try to toss me a bone. "Now, this is a fine young man here," he'd say. "You make sure you treat him right."

There was a party for George the next evening at the pavilion in the town square. When Rebecca and I left the house to walk to the event, we could see there were streams of people doing the same thing. It seemed the whole town was there that night, and the party stretched well past midnight, as we heard dozens of Manchesterians get up and pay tribute to their favorite mailman.

"He sure is loved," Rebecca whispered in my ear. "You've got some big shoes to fill, Paul Bennett."

I nodded, although I wanted to tell her that I had no intention of filling any mailman's shoes. I was going to be a writer; toting a postal bag was a temporary gig until my dream kicked in. I thought about reminding my wife of this, but let it pass.

◆ ◆ ◆

While I walked my freshman route and set out to win the hearts of George's former mail customers, Rebecca began refurbishing our new/old house. For several weeks in the late summer of our first year in Manchester, I'd come home each evening, and she'd be wearing a backward painter's cap, her cheeks, hair, and coveralls splotched with paint.

"Honey, did you manage to get any of that paint on the walls today?" I'd ask, and she'd pretend to be offended.

"Oh, stop it. I'm doing an awesome job."

And she was. In short order, Becca transformed the dreary house interior into a bright and welcoming family home. It was as if she'd taken a pail of warmth and slapped it on the walls and trim.

Evenings and weekends, I'd be by her side, sanding and sawing, hammering and painting. Neighbors like the Yagers from across the street or the Mathewsons from next door would wander by from time to time, bringing fresh pies and casseroles. They all seemed thrilled that the dilapidated old place, after years of neglect, was finally getting a facelift.

"The old girl's come alive again," Gary Yager said one morning as he stood at our gate with his dog, Fritzy, on leash. And he was right.

In about six weeks' time we had the house on Bethlehem Place in pretty good shape, and while I thought we needed a little break from our fixer-upping, the lady of the house had other ideas.

"Okay! On to stage two!" Rebecca said. "Landscaping. Time's a-wasting!"

Considering winter came early in northern Maine, she had a good point. We'd have to hustle to beat the first snowfall, but my wife wouldn't be deterred. She had an artist's vision about our new home and would not rest until it came to fruition.

As soon as our neighbors saw us working in the yard, they appeared with hoes and mattocks, rakes and shovels. They knew we'd need extra hands if we were to beat the approaching winter. Our yard soon became something of a community garden as our new friends helped us breathe life into the drab grounds. Before long, our property was rife with native wildflowers like crimson clover, purple loosestrife, and fringed orchids, along with dogwood and eastern white pine trees. And there was Rebecca, directing the operation like a green-thumbed General Patton.

Once the outside was finished and we'd transformed the grounds into a page right out of *Better Homes and Gardens*, my single-minded wife turned her focus back inside to the little upstairs parlor room. She set about converting it into her art studio, complete with easel and palette, brushes and paint.

The view from the art-room window offered endless and ever-changing landscape themes: a nest of robins in spring, a potpourri of bright colors in summer, the deep red and golden leaves of autumn, and a gray fox looking out from snow-covered woods in the dead of winter.

Becca would sit in that cozy little room for hours on end painting watercolor landscapes and singing along to her favorite music on the stereo: Frank Sinatra and Nat King Cole, Carly Simon and James Taylor.

For Rebecca, her paints were far more than a pastime. Painting was her passion.

"I love the blank canvas almost as much as the completed painting," she said. "I love its promise."

Whenever I'd stop by her art studio to say hello or bring her a cup of coffee or tea, I'd find Becca perched in front of the easel, brush in hand, and no matter the weather outside, the window would always be open. On most days, you could hear the giddy voices of neighborhood children floating through the woods and into our home.

"I love the sound of children laughing," Rebecca said one autumn afternoon. She looked at me and smiled, and I knew what she was thinking. She was ready to hear that laughter a little closer to home.

"Do you know Karen Gates?" Rebecca said. It was two weeks before Christmas, and we were in the den trimming our very first married-couple Christmas tree.

"Sure," I said. "She owns the art gallery on the square."

"Well . . ." Rebecca said. "I ran into her in the market yesterday, and she got me talking about my paintings and . . . one thing led to another." Rebecca stepped back from the tree. "Sweetie, do you think that's enough tinsel?"

"Becca, don't do that."

"Do what?"

"Change the subject."

Rebecca smiled. "Well . . . Karen asked to see some of my work, and I took a couple of landscapes down to her today, and . . . she liked them."

"Meaning . . . ?" I said.

"She wants to put them in her gallery."

"Honey, that's great!" I gave her a hug and sprinkled a smattering of silver tinsel on her fire-red hair.

"Yeah," she said. "I have to admit—I'm a little excited. Do you think I might actually be able to sell one?"

"What are you talking about?" I said. "They're going to sell like hotcakes. Where does that expression come from anyway? *Sell like hotcakes.*" Rebecca gave me a kiss on the chin.

"Pretty cool, huh?" she said. I brushed a stray hair from her cheek.

"Totally cool. I'm so proud of you."

My enthusiasm was sincere, but I had to admit, I was a little worried. What if nobody wanted to buy her paintings? How would Rebecca handle that? Fortunately, I never had to find out. Three days after the first Rebecca Anne Waverly original was displayed in the window of Gates Artworks, it sold to an out-of-towner from Boston. A week later, she sold another landscape. Soon, the gallery was selling Becca's paintings almost as soon as the paint dried.

"You're my little Monet," I said to her one night as we slipped into bed. "Pretty soon you'll be too famous to be married to a mailman."

"You're probably right," she said as she fluffed her pillow. "But, then again, I do need someone to deliver my fan mail."

Rebecca was hooked. Painting as a hobby was one thing, but actually selling her works and making a little scratch—she was in artist's heaven. Within three months, she'd sold seven paintings and had orders for four more. My Becca had turned her passion for art into a business, and she was proud to call herself a professional artiste.

◆　◆　◆

From her painter's perch on the second floor, Rebecca looked down on the backyard shed we'd renovated for use as my "writer's shack." Her little second-story gallery was her creative corner, and the shed was mine. It was there, in that delightfully cramped space, I spent evenings and lazy weekend afternoons plunking away on that old-timey Underwood typewriter.

I was working on my first novel—a tragic and melancholy story set against the backdrop of World War II. It was a romance with lots of untimely death and tragedy and the overcoming of impossible odds so that love could triumph in the end. I was sure it would one day win a Pulitzer—that is, if I ever finished it. My debut book was quickly becoming a never-ending opus, a meandering tale of love and loss that leisurely drifted on and on with no discernible end in sight.

"How's the book coming, and when do I get to read it?" she'd say almost weekly. She was genuinely curious, but also probably wondering why in the world it was taking so long. She could knock out a half-dozen paintings before I could muster one short chapter.

The truth was, I had no idea when I'd be finished, so I'd hem and haw and evade her question. The thought of trying to fashion a sensible ending terrified me. What if it was the wrong ending? What if I found there really was no sensible way to bring my story to conclusion?

A few times, I thought about tossing the manuscript out the window and starting over. All too often, I'd stare at the paper in the typewriter with not a clue what to type. I comforted my indecisive psyche by telling myself that was how the great ones wrote—a few words at a time. I pretended that the likes of Thomas Wolfe, F. Scott Fitzgerald, and Charlotte Brontë all had their own doubts and reservations, though I had no idea if that were true. Deep down, I was afraid I'd ventured out of my literary depth. What if my entire story was simply no good? What if no one cared about my characters and their dilemmas? What if I'd been wasting trees sitting out there in my writer's hideaway? Still, I plugged away. Rebecca was waiting.

Weeks and months passed, and I wore through a half-dozen old typewriter ribbons one by one. Pages mounted on the shed floor, crumpled and rejected, giving way to new pages that somehow, at first, seemed an improvement—only to soon join the paper junkyard on the floor. Bit by bit the pages came, but I had no confidence I was writing anything near worthy of Rebecca Waverly. After all, she was brilliant. She got into Yale. And what if I let her read a few pages—a chapter maybe—and she didn't like it? Becca wasn't a very good actress, and I'd be able to read the disapproval on her face. And so I wrote on and on and kept putting her off. It had to be perfect.

"Love the process," my high school English teacher Mrs. Hansen once said. And I did. I loved the feel of the vintage keys against my fingertips, the *clickety-clop* of metal striking paper. It relaxed me. When I was out in my shed plunking away on that old typewriter, I could imagine I was, in some small and distant way, connected to the great New England writers of a bygone era. Thoreau. Alcott. Emerson. Rebecca had her paints; I had my words. And so what if I took forever to finish? At least I was having fun. And then I'd look out the dusty shed window and see Rebecca sitting up in her artist's perch. She'd turn to me as if she could feel my gaze, smile, blow me a kiss, and for a brief moment in two young romantic lives, all would be right with the world.

CHAPTER ELEVEN

One cool early April evening, as we neared the first anniversary of our arrival in Manchester, I came home from work to discover Rebecca wasn't in her art studio.

"Becca?"

"I'm in here."

I followed her voice down the upstairs hall to the small bedroom we'd been using for storage. All the boxes had been moved from the center of the room and were stacked in one corner. Rebecca was perched on a mini stepladder, clad in coveralls and painter's cap, paint-sodden roller in hand. I smelled the fresh coat of primer.

"Babe, what are you doing?" I said.

Rebecca hopped down and gave me a kiss.

"Getting a jump start."

I gave her my puzzled face. "Jump start . . . on what?"

She went back to painting. "On getting the room ready, of course."

"Okay," I said. "Ready for what?"

"Our new arrival. Soon as we find out the sex we can choose a color. That is—unless you want to wait and be surprised. Then we can go neutral." She smiled at the stupefied look on my face and rubbed her belly. "Congratulations, Daddy."

Megan Elisabeth Bennett arrived a week early, at 12:25 a.m. on Thursday, November 28, the morning of our second Thanksgiving in Manchester. And, yes, we had a lot to be grateful for that year—specifically a seven-pound, three-ounce, green-eyed bundle with lovely cherry locks—just like her mother. My first call was to Pops. I could hear the sheer joy in his voice as he joked about what he wanted to be called by his freshly printed granddaughter. "I prefer Pawpaw," he said. "Or Grampa Hank." Pops said he was taking the morning train and would be cradling his granddaughter before she was a day old. He promised to call when he left the house.

When we hadn't heard from him by eleven the next morning, I called him. The phone kept ringing. Pops didn't believe in voice mail or an answering machine, and he thought cell phones were silly. My next call was to the Urgos next door. Mr. Urgo promised to check on him. He later told me he found Pops sitting in the easy chair in the living room, dead from a heart attack, the phone near his feet. We figured he'd died right after hanging up from speaking with me the previous evening. His neighbor said my father had the "sweetest little smile on his face."

I drove to the city as soon as I found out, and Rebecca's mother jumped on a plane to Manchester to help her daughter with the baby. For the next few weeks, I felt the strangest mix of grief and euphoria—devastated by the loss of my dad, yet overjoyed at the arrival of our little girl. I wondered if God had planned it that way, so that I'd have the strength to handle it. I was grateful that the last earthly thought that must have gone through Pops' mind was of his first granddaughter. His loss was still hard on me, and as time would tell, he wouldn't be there for me—when I needed him most.

◆ ◆ ◆

By the time little Meg arrived, we'd long since transformed the small room next to Becca's art studio into a girlie-girl bedroom with lavender curtains, butterfly wallpaper, and half a dozen very large stuffed bears. And no, we didn't ask about the sex during any of our ultrasounds. Becca had gone with her grandmother's unscientific yet accurate advice: if the bump is riding high on the expectant mom, it's gonna be a girl. I had a couple cans of blue latex paint hidden in the shed in case she was wrong. Rebecca never knew.

The instant we saw Megan, Rebecca and I fell in love all over again. Almost from the moment she arrived in the world, Baby Meg loved to stare. She would stare at the sky and the ceiling, the faucet in the bathtub, trees and flowers—and she would gaze up at us with her huge searching eyes as if to say *"What do you think you're looking at?"*

She was a month old on her first Christmas and spent it wriggling on a blanket in front of our six-foot Douglas fir Christmas tree. The Yagers stopped by with a tiny homemade wooden "Megan" tree ornament, and Pastor Joe Moody and his wife, Erin, brought us a classic black vintage baby stroller that looked like it was lifted from a Mary Poppins garage sale. There was a steady stream of neighbors and friends and postal customers dropping by with gifts and food and well wishes. We heard from friends that Meg was an *easy* baby, though we had no basis for comparison. All we knew was she hardly ever cried and almost always slept through the night.

"She's going to spoil us, you know," Rebecca said one night as we tucked little Meggy in her crib. "If we ever decide to have another." Becca often used the "if we ever decide to have another" phrase, which, of course, meant she really *wanted* to have another.

Before Meg had even turned three, Rebecca had our curious little cherub poised on a drafting chair in front of her own mini canvas. I would come home from work and find my daughter covered head to toe with a rainbow of watercolor paint. She would greet me at the bottom of the stairs with a big grin on her face, clutching her latest masterpiece.

"Hee-yah, Daddy. I paint fuh you."

I would accept her humble gift as if I'd been awarded the *Mona Lisa* for my personal collection. Then, with my miniature Mary Cassatt toddling close behind, I'd march straight to the kitchen and magnet her work of art to the fridge next to the others.

"I always knew she was an artist," Rebecca said one Friday evening as we listened to Meg sing while she brushed her teeth. "The way she was always looking at things when she was a baby. She's so curious about everything."

"Who knows?" I said. "Maybe she'll be a writer."

Sensing I felt slighted, Rebecca began to nudge little Meg out to visit me on Saturday afternoons, while I typed away on my never-ending masterpiece. She'd patter out back to the writer's shack and climb up in my lap. I loved watching her little face, transfixed on the methodically clicking typewriter keys as if she were witnessing a magic show.

Usually, I'd give up on getting any real writing done, pull out the manuscript, and roll in a blank sheet of paper for Megan to mess around with. Maybe her mother had introduced her to the joys of putting paint to canvas, but her dad taught her how to type her first words. It was times like those that my novel didn't seem so important anymore. I had a beautiful wife and daughter whom I loved more than anything in the world, and a life that felt . . . perfect. And though it didn't seem possible, it was about to get even better.

Abigail Rose Bennett came along nearly four years to the day after her big sister. She showed up with blond hair and big lungs. Abbey popped out screaming and kept at it for a good two hours before she drifted off for her first nap. As soon as our newborn's eyes closed and we could tell she was asleep, Rebecca and I looked at each other.

"Our easy-baby payment has come due," Becca said.

Where Megan had been a walk in the baby park, Abbey was a walk on the baby wild side. She cried when she woke up, when you picked her up, and when you put her down. She cried when you'd look at her, and when you'd look away. She cried on rainy days, when it was sunny and partly cloudy. She cried at loud noises and at the lack of noise. Sometimes she cried and we couldn't put our fingers on any discernible reason at all. She just liked to cry. It seemed the only one who could get her to stop was Pastor Joe. Abbey would be wailing away, her face as red as a cherry tomato, but as soon as our minister took her in his arms, the crying would shut off like a faucet. She'd smile at him until her little eyelids grew heavy and she drifted off to sleep. It was almost eerie.

"Can you come live with us?" I asked Pastor Joe one particularly trying Sunday morning.

"Yes!" Rebecca said. "We'll sleep on the couch, and you can have our bedroom."

Baby Abbey's sleep pattern wasn't really a pattern at all. Some nights she got in a good eight hours, while other nights had her waking up five to six times.

"I told you the bill would come due," Rebecca said. It was two in the morning, and Abbey was crying yet again. I was so groggy from lack of sleep I felt drunk. "But she's a cute little bill, isn't she?"

Pastor Joe had assured us that our sleepless nights would only be temporary, but at the time, it seemed our youngest daughter was destined to be a cranky little bugger her whole life. However, by the time Abbey turned three, Joe's prophecy had come to pass. She'd mercifully come out of her indiscriminate crying phase and morphed into a real little girl with opinions and funny sayings and a goofy cackle laugh. And she was an independent little nugget.

"I wanna do it myself!" was her most common refrain.

And she idolized her "Meggy." Abbey followed big sis around like a devoted puppy, traipsing after her all over the house and yard and neighborhood. Megan adored her little sister, but she could only stand the idol worship for so long.

"I need some space!" Meg would bark. Then little Abbey's cheeks would flush pink, and her moon-shaped brown eyes well up with tears. Megan always gave in. She couldn't stand to see her little sister cry.

"We have so much to be grateful for" was Rebecca's favorite saying, and she wanted to make sure the girls remembered not only to give thanks—but also to give back. We made regular trips to the animal shelter to wash the stray dogs, and each Sunday afternoon, we'd stop by the local nursing home to play backgammon, Parcheesi, and checkers with the senior residents.

We Bennetts of Bethlehem Place had carved out a nice little slice of heaven in lovely Manchester—a town that had gradually grown on me over our few years there. As the months and years passed, the old hard-line postal customers, who would sometimes comment how much they missed George, finally came to accept "the new kid" as one of their own. And even though I wasn't planning on delivering mail for the rest of my life, I actually enjoyed my work. I got to be outdoors, talk to people, and take advantage of little old ladies who lived to share their latest batch of homemade cookies and lemonade.

"It's a good thing you get to exercise with your job," Rebecca said. "With all that between-meal-eating you do."

And church was at the center of our lives.

Rebecca had grown up church-hopping all over Manhattan. Jack and Jane Waverly saw churchgoing as a social exercise, an opportunity to see and be seen by those in the upper crust of New York society. While her parents were craning their necks in the pews, young Rebecca was actually listening to the sermons. Her spiritually fertile young mind drank in the words from the pulpit, and she soon discovered that there were as many views on God and theology as there were ministers. She loved most of the passages of scripture and kept a well-worn Bible on her nightstand with notes in the margins.

Rebecca found that reading the Good Book at night helped her relax. Her favorite passage was from Isaiah.

Fear thou not; for I am with thee: be not dismayed; for I am thy God: I will strengthen thee; yea, I will help thee; yea, I will uphold thee with the right hand of my righteousness.

I'd never been much of a churchgoer growing up—at least not after Mom died. She'd been the one who had insisted that Pops and I get up on Sunday morning, put on our finest coat and tie, and walk the five blocks to the Methodist church. It was a monumental effort prying my father out of bed, especially after he'd driven all night in his cab, but Mom thought it was important.

"We owe God at least an hour on Sunday," she'd say whenever our sleepy protests would reach a crescendo. Though Pops loved his sleep, he loved his Claire even more, so he'd roll out of bed and roust me up.

"C'mon, son. Your mom's trying to save our souls."

As a boy, I found sitting still in a pew listening to some man talk about something I didn't understand nearly insufferable. But whenever I'd fidget a little too much, my mother would clasp my hand in hers and give me a little squeeze. That was the part I remembered most about Sunday church: sitting there on that hard bench with my mother's hand wrapped around mine. It was that feeling of warmth and comfort, of being loved, that I carried with me long after she was gone.

After Mom died, Pops tried his best to keep up her Sunday morning routine, but his desire to sleep in on Sundays won out, and I sure wouldn't go by myself. I suppose, because of my lack of a lasting spiritual foundation, I had a rather open-ended view of religion. Rebecca found that curious.

"Do you believe in God?" She asked me the question on our very first evening stroll at Camp Arrowhead.

"I don't believe or not believe," I said. "Truth is . . . I don't give him much thought."

"I don't get it," Rebecca said. "How can you not think about God?"

I didn't have an answer. Deep down, maybe I blamed the big man in the sky for taking my mom from me, and it was easier to ignore him than deal with how I felt about that. However, from nearly the moment Rebecca came into my life, our God talks became frequent occurrences, and as much as I tried to steer the conversation in a different direction, Rebecca wouldn't let me change the subject.

"Paul, don't you get it?" she said. "A world without God wouldn't be worth living in at all. How can you look at all the wonders around you and not ponder God?"

Rebecca was a firm believer and a deep thinker—though she didn't subscribe to any particular religious doctrine. Despite her Ivy League intellect, Becca's belief system was simple and childlike.

"I believe in a loving God who's always watching over me. And I know he believes in me, too."

She let me know well ahead of our marriage that she wanted church to be an important part of our life together. Even though she never actually came out and said it, I felt that it was a deal breaker. A life with Rebecca Waverly would mean no more sleeping in on Sunday mornings. Since I was mostly ambivalent about God and religion, I had no objection. I figured I could go through the church motions if that was what she wanted. But I knew that no amount of churchgoing was going to change how I felt in my heart. God was a dubious being to me, and I figured he always would be.

Up to the day Rebecca entered my world, I'd prayed exactly two times in my life. Both prayers—humble and awkward as they were—took place the night my mother died. In the first prayer, I prayed that God wouldn't take her. It was really just an exercise in begging and pleading and bargaining, as I hadn't a clue how a prayer was supposed to go. I offered up that I would no longer shoplift bubble gum from Jolly's convenience store on the way home from school. I threw in a moratorium on swearing—even though, up to that point, my dirty words were pretty mild. I believed those to be fair bargaining chips for my mother's life. After Mom died, I figured that my offerings had fallen short, so I simply prayed that God would take care of her in heaven. I asked that he please admit her forthwith and that she not have to go through any prolonged application process. And then I tagged on one more request before saying amen.

"Dear God, please don't let my mother forget me."

CHAPTER TWELVE

"Gratitude is much more than just words," our young pastor, Joe Moody, said one Sunday morning. "It is the cornerstone of humankind."

Rebecca and I had found our way to Manchester Christian Church on our very first Sunday in town. We felt at home the moment we plopped down on the left side, fourth pew from the front. The church was vintage New England, with a creaky wooden plank floor and equally creaky handmade benches. The parishioners welcomed us with smiles and hugs, and we were happy to see there were several other young couples.

Pastor Joe himself was only thirty-four and, like us, a relative newcomer to Manchester. He and his wife, Erin, had moved up from Pennsylvania three years before we arrived. Our new clergyman was enthusiastic, energetic, and brimming with hope. He was also a master storyteller, and we were hooked from the very first sermon. He had several signature lines that I always looked forward to—even if I wasn't so sure I understood or believed them.

"Sometimes you get all worked up over a Camry when God has a Mercedes in mind for you all along."

"What you are seeking is also seeking you."

"Draw near to God in your hearts, and he will draw near to you."

"Peace be still."

Joe Moody's early life did in no way forecast a career in the ministry. As a matter of fact, the circumstances of his life as a teenager didn't even guarantee he would make it to adulthood. He was an only child, and his alcoholic petty-crook father liked to tell Joe that he was a "drunken mistake" whenever the boy got in trouble at school—which was nearly every day. The Moody family of three lived in a double-wide in Sharon, Pennsylvania, near the truck-stop diner where his mother worked as a waitress. While his father's abuse was verbal for most of Joe's early boyhood, it turned physical about the time he turned eight. His father rarely, if ever, worked and was home all day on the couch drinking and watching television. His mother, Jeannie, took as many shifts as she could to keep the Moodys' heads just above water. Jeannie pushed Joe to succeed at school as best she knew how, but she didn't have the time or the energy to stay on top of him all the time.

One day, in fourth grade, Joe came home from school to find that his father had moved out. He later described it in a sermon as the "best worst day of his life." He waited up past midnight until his mother returned from her waitress shift to tell her. He remembered she'd said little.

"She went to the refrigerator, popped open a bottle of beer, and took a swig that looked a lot to me like relief," Joe said.

With little to no parental supervision in his life, Joe was bound to get into trouble. And beginning in seventh grade, he really started going off the disciplinary rails. His slide started out with small things, like setting off the school fire alarm and skipping class to smoke with his friends, later escalating to back-talking teachers and shoving the PE coach. He was expelled four months into eighth grade for lighting a fire in the boys' bathroom. By that time, his mother was pregnant by a long-gone trucker whose name she didn't even know.

"Hope my baby doesn't turn out like you," Jeannie Moody told Joe. She was crying when she said it, and Joe knew that her words came more from heartbreak than mean-spiritedness. It still hurt, so

Joe shoved his few possessions into a duffel and moved in with a fellow expellee named Bobby Case. Bobby was two years older, and his family was even worse off than Joe's. Both his parents were in prison, and he was living in an uncle's basement while the uncle dealt drugs upstairs. Bobby would lead Joe into the darkest time of his life.

"When you're cast in darkness," Pastor Joe once said, "there's only one way to go—and that's toward the light."

Bobby told Joe of a convenience store he'd been casing for weeks. An old man who worked the Sunday night graveyard shift looked, according to Bobby, like "a good stiff wind would blow him over."

"Easy take," Bobby told Joe one night. The boys were sitting in an open boxcar down at the railroad yard smoking homemade cigarettes. Joe was fifteen years old. "We walk in wearing ski masks, scare the old codger, and clean out the register," Bobby said. "We'll be in and out in less than a minute. And the best thing is . . . there ain't nobody around that time of night."

"How do we scare him?" Joe said.

"My uncle has a pistol," Bobby said. "Fool keeps it under his bed. I can swipe it, and he'll never know."

Joe took a long drag on his cigarette as he considered this venture into armed robbery. He had one question. "How do we split the cash?"

◆ ◆ ◆

Erin Amber Williams, who would one day lead Joe Moody through the darkest days of his life, grew up the daughter of a Baptist preacher in Elizabethtown, Pennsylvania. Her father, Amos, had the same midsized congregation he'd inherited from his father, Thomas. Amos had been known to say that he loved his only daughter only slightly less than he loved the Lord. Erin was the apple of the reverend's eye, but he knew that preachers' daughters sometimes had a reputation for rebellion. He'd seen the daughters of his colleagues run amok and sometimes even end up diving right off the deep end. Amos had a theory that this happened because their daddies sheltered them from the sharper edges in life, keeping them on a tight leash so as not to be an embarrassment to their pious parents. So when Erin turned fifteen, he decided on a preemptive strike. He sent her to prison.

"That's what I like to tell people," Erin Moody once told her Sunday school class. "It always gets their attention."

In reality, she was put on what they called the Church Institutions Committee, a group of some two dozen church members who visited prisons and delivered literature and met with inmates. As the youngest member of the committee, Erin was assigned, along with four others, to a juvenile facility nearby in Lancaster County, where, by that time, one Joe Moody had been cooling his heels for nearly two years.

The convenience-store robbery had not gone as hitch free as Bobby had forecast. Turns out the old man was an ex-Marine who'd been awarded the Silver Star in Korea. He kept a Colt semiautomatic service pistol stowed in a drawer beneath the cash register.

He was watching when the boys emerged from the woods across from the store, and he could see them put on their ski masks as they passed beneath the streetlight. When they came through the door of the Qwik Stop convenience store, the old cashier was nowhere to be found. An easy score—or so they thought.

Joe kept lookout by the front door while Bobby jumped the counter and tried to jimmy the register. That was when the old guy emerged from his hiding place, pistol aimed right at Bobby's head.

"You can meet your maker tonight or later," the old man said. "The choice is yours."

Joe could have run but figured there was no point. The old guy held the boys at gunpoint until the sheriff and a half-dozen deputies arrived. Bobby got five years in big-boy prison. But as a first-time youth offender, fifteen-year-old Joe was given thirty months in a juvenile detention center. At the hearing, Joe's mother showed up drunk and told the judge she didn't care what happened to him. "I never want to lay eyes on you again," she said to Joe. And she never did.

Erin met Joe on a Saturday morning in the visiting area of the Lancaster County Youth Intervention Center. She'd been assigned to him randomly by the prison liaison. He didn't even look at her when she sat across from him.

"You're wasting your time," he said. "I don't believe in God."

It was Erin's very first time in a facility, and Joe was her first inmate. Her father had given her advice as she was walking out the door that morning. "Don't try to sell them. Just let your light shine."

Erin took a moment, gathered her thoughts, and said the first thing that came to mind. "Yeah? Well, I don't blame you."

Joe looked up and saw her for the first time—a pretty, bright-eyed, brown-haired girl sitting across from him, a copy of the Holy Bible on the table next to her. He later spoke of that moment in a sermon on the power of marriage.

"I knew at that moment that I wanted to be with that girl. Now, I was locked up at the time, mind you, so I couldn't figure out the logistics of it all, but I knew one thing for sure—I wanted to spend the rest of my life with her."

And just like that, for the first time in his life, Joe Moody had something to look forward to. He decided he could bear any hardship, live through any indignity, as long as he knew he'd see Erin sitting across from him Saturday morning. He was even willing to hear about God, if that's what she wanted to talk about. But much to his surprise, Erin didn't talk about God at all.

"Now, I have to admit," Joe said. "She played me perfectly. She never once brought up God or religion or saving. She talked about movies and music and sports, asked me questions about what I liked and didn't like. I was waiting for the proselytizing, the 'You'd better get right with the Lord or else' talk. But it never came. She didn't talk about the Lord at all—until *I* brought it up. One Saturday morning I decided I'd try to stump her.

"'Okay, church girl. If you had to define your God in one word, what word would you use?'

"She smiled. 'Well, first of all, he's not just *my* God. He's yours and everybody else's, too. And I think if I had to pick one word I'd pick . . . love.'

"Erin said she chose love because it's the most beautiful word in the English language and—even though it was totally inadequate to capture the greatness of God—it was the best word she could think of.

"'God is love,' she said. 'And God loves you, Joe. As soon as you accept that, there's nothing in the world you can't accomplish. You can change. You can turn your life around.'

"I remember that the guard came in after that and said it was time for Erin to leave. I wanted so badly to go with her, to talk to her some more about God, to try and get some answers to the questions that were swirling in my head. That next week I stretched out on my bunk for hours on end thinking about the idea that God loved me. I figured if she was right, and if God truly loved me, then maybe he had a plan for my life that didn't involve sitting in some stale cramped jail cell. And then it dawned on me—because God loved me, I could never really be incarcerated. Knowing that was my freedom. There I was in my cell all alone in the middle of the night, and I was having this experience—a spiritual transformation. I realized that, as God's child, I was already free, that I could be free in my heart and soul and mind, even if my body was locked in an iron cage.

"From that moment on, I was a changed man. I woke up the next morning, and some of the guards didn't even recognize me. The scowl was gone, the surliness and cynicism. The anger. The warden was so alarmed by my change, he dragged me in for drug testing. And when Erin returned the next Saturday, she could tell right away I was a different person. Three weeks after that, I was released, about three months earlier than expected. I turned eighteen the next day and hitched a ride to Elizabethtown to be near Erin. Her father gave me a job helping out around the church, cutting grass and keeping the place up. Of course, Reverend Amos took me aside and had the *talk*.

"'There will be no dating my daughter until she turns eighteen. Do you understand me, son?'

"'Yes sir, Pops,' I said. 'I sure wish she'd hurry up, though.'

"Reverend Williams was known as a serious, no-nonsense man, but I guess there was something about the way I said it that struck him as funny. He threw back his head and laughed and then tousled my hair. 'I'll be watching you, boy,' he said. 'And God's watching you, too.'

"Erin and I had our first date on her eighteenth birthday, and we've been together ever since. Sometimes, I think getting tossed in juvy was the best thing that ever happened to me. Actually, I know it was. It changed my life."

Pastor Joe would always finish the story of how he and Erin came to be with the account of Shadrach, Meshach, and Abednego from the Book of Daniel.

"*'He answered and said, Lo, I see four men loose, walking in the midst of the fire, and they have no hurt; and the form of the fourth is like the Son of God.'* Those three men stood up for their convictions," Pastor Joe said. "And because they put God first, they were protected in that fiery furnace. If we stand with God, my friends, he will stand with us."

◆ ◆ ◆

Every Sunday morning, Rebecca would dress the girls, do their hair up nice, and we'd walk the four blocks to church. Ever the well-behaved little angel, Megan sat quietly and listened to Pastor Joe's sermon while Abbey squirmed and fidgeted and held loudly whispered conversations with her imaginary friends and her imaginary friends' friends. We tried at first to keep her quiet, but eventually gave up. I sometimes caught myself tuning out the pastor and looking at my wife. She'd close her eyes as she listened to the sermon, blocking out all distractions. Her face always had such a sweet and peaceful expression when she was in church. I'd watch her and wonder how in the world I got so lucky to end up with someone so extraordinary. Sometimes, as if she could feel my eyes on her, she'd glance my way and smile. I'd smile back at her and then turn my attention to Pastor Joe again to catch up.

Rebecca wanted to make sure the girls knew that church was not just a Sunday thing. Each night at bedtime, as we tucked the girls in, we'd have them list three things they had to be grateful for that day. Meg and Abbey called it the "grateful game" and attacked it with gusto. They usually had a hard time narrowing it down to three, and their gratitude list would end up being a dozen or more long. We came to suspect that they used the game to delay "lights out" at long as possible.

"I'm afraid," Rebecca said to me one night as we slipped into bed. We were coming up on our eleventh Christmas in Manchester. Megan was nine, and Abbey had just turned five. Miraculously, my endless manuscript was nearing completion, I'd gotten a raise at the post office, and Rebecca was still selling her watercolor paintings as fast as she could finish them.

"What are you afraid of?" I said.

"Our life seems too perfect," she said. "For some reason, that scares me."

I kissed her forehead, leaned over, and switched off the bedside lamp. "Maybe this is the happily ever after," I said. "And we don't even realize it."

◆ ◆ ◆

I had spotted the white-leather vintage ice skates in the window of Walker Sporting Goods the previous morning, and even though Becca and I had wound up our Christmas shopping a week earlier, I decided to get them for Megan. She'd loved ice-skating since the first time I took her out on Waller's Pond the winter of her second year. I'd held her tiny mittened hands, put her little feet on top of my skates, and gently guided her across the ice. Her face lit up as she glided for the first time.

Soon after, Meg had her own mini skates, and let me know in no uncertain terms, "I don't need anybody's help." Skating became her joy. Each winter Saturday morning, she'd wake up with one passion in mind. "I want to go skating. Daddy, will you take me?" And despite my groaning and excuse-making, I'd usually cave. And we always had fun. Many times, Megan's friends would be there, and I'd end up sitting on a bench with the other parents watching our kids cut circles in the ice and play hockey. Megan was a pure joy to watch. She was a natural on skates and seemed her happiest when she was on the ice.

And, as much as she loved skating, Megan loved Christmas even more—an affection she passed down to her little sister. Our house was especially festive that Christmas season. We'd barely put away the Thanksgiving leftovers when Rebecca presented me with her "Holiday Lighting Schematic." She confessed she'd been secretly working on it since summer, and laid out a plan to turn our house into a green-and-red Christmas extravaganza the likes of which the neighborhood had never seen.

"Honey, it's Christmas," I said. "Not a competition."

She gave me a pinch on the arm. "You're just saying that so you won't have to do the work."

She was right. It took three weeks' worth of evenings and weekends to complete Rebecca's grand design that year—a complex, intricate lighting motif that at first seemed a bit arbitrary. Only when I was nearly finished stringing and stretching the dozens of strands of lights did her vision come into focus. Once again, my artist wife knew exactly what she was doing.

When I finished, we blindfolded the girls with scarves, led them outside, and held our Bennett Family Official Christmas Decorations

House Lighting. I felt a little like Chevy Chase in *Christmas Vacation*; luckily, when I flipped the switch, we didn't short out the fuse box.

Standing there in front of our house that late December evening, arms around my three girls, I had to admit—we owned the neighborhood.

Our picket fence was strung with classic white icicle lights; there was a red "North Pole" sign affixed to the top of the mailbox. Parked on the roof was a cherry-nosed Rudolph leading the famous team of eight glowing plastic reindeer. An especially rotund Santa Claus was emerging from the chimney with his red felt sack slung over his shoulder. Spread out on the lawn was a nativity scene, complete with hay and a handmade wooden manger. The front porch railing was lined with silk poinsettias, and red and green twinkle lights snaked around the posts, accented by a large holly wreath on the front door.

From the street, passersby could see the glimmering spruce Christmas tree in the window, crowned with a metallic silver star and lots of tinsel because that's how Megan and Abbey liked it.

The inside was pretty cool, too. The living room crackled with holiday spirit—from the four red stockings lining the mantel to the holiday favorites spinning on the vintage record player Becca picked up for five bucks at McGregor's Antique Store. There were a few dozen smartly wrapped gifts of all shapes and sizes beneath the tree.

When I left the post office to head out on my rounds that Christmas Eve, the thought of all the festivities waiting for me at home put a spring in my step. That year, Christmas Eve morning was blue and clear and unseasonably warm for northern Maine. Temps were hovering a few degrees above freezing when I left the post office to head out on my rounds.

I was humming "Angels We Have Heard on High" as I crossed the square. I always dropped off the merchant mail before moving on to my residential customers, so my first stop was Walker Sporting Goods at the corner of Fourth and Main. Mr. Hal Walker was opening for the day as I walked up. I had his mail ready. He was a second-generation storeowner. His father, Philip, had opened the store when he returned home from World War II. Though there was a steady stream of customers, Hal made most of his money supplying jerseys and equipment for Manchester high and middle schools. The younger Walker was nearing sixty years old and could be a little brusque and off-putting to those who didn't know him. His wife, Jemma, called him "Old Man Curmudgeon." I liked him, and he liked me. He always asked about Rebecca and the girls, and would give me updates on his five kids—all of whom were grown up and gone. Then he'd throw in a comment about how none of them wanted to stay home and take over the family business. Though he'd never come right out and admit it, I could tell this disappointed him.

"I've got nobody to give this place to," he'd sometimes say. He'd make a joke of it and laugh it off, but I knew it hurt. He'd devoted his life to what was his father's dream, yet his children had dreams of their own.

Hal Walker was an ex-jock who lived and breathed sports. He was a local football hero who, as an all-Maine running back in the mid-1970s, had led Manchester to their one and only trip to the state playoffs. He still had a bit of the old swagger.

"Merry Christmas, Hal," I said and held out his stack of letters.

"Hello, Paul. How are those pretty girls of yours?"

"They're great. How's Jemma?"

"I tell you, Paul. You and me are two of the luckiest guys in the whole state of Maine. Tell me. How'd two ugly mugs like us end up with two beauties like that?"

"Good question," I said. "Wish I had a good answer."

Walker took his mail and checked the sky. "Hear it may hit forty today."

"Suits me," I said. I looked at the store window and noticed the white-leather skates on display. They were old school, like something

Sonja Henie might have worn at Lake Placid. I knew in an instant Meg would love them.

"What time do you close this evening?" I said.

"Six sharp," Walker said.

I did the time calculation in my head. It was Christmas Eve, so my usual timing would be a bit off. Six would be cutting it close, but it was doable if I skipped lunch. "I'm coming back for those skates," I said.

Walker smiled. "For Megan?"

I grinned. "A last-minute gift. She's going to love 'em."

"I'll put 'em away for you," Walker said. "Knock off ten percent. That'll be your Christmas gift."

"Deal," I said. "Don't worry. I'll be back for them."

"Don't be late," Walker said. "Jemma said I'd best be home on time this evening—or else."

◆ ◆ ◆

It was a typically busy Christmas Eve day, and I had to make several trips back to the post office to pick up more holiday mail as late deliveries trickled in. As expected, I was running over an hour behind, which meant I reached the final house on my route a few minutes before six.

My last customer also happened to be my oldest and most verbose. Mrs. Evelyn Clarke had been a widow longer than she'd been married. She lived in Manchester her whole life—well over eighty years. When she was born in the early 1930s, Main Street was a dirt road and the town square just a couple of stores, a bar, and a greasy spoon. There were fewer than four hundred people living there.

After her husband, Luther, died in the early 1970s, Mrs. Clarke had two great loves left in life: gardening and talking. My mail-carrying predecessor, George, had warned me that Old Lady C liked to "bend your ear a bit." She readily admitted she was a little nervous about the "new boy," as she called me in the months following George's retirement. But I soon won her over by spending a few minutes on her porch listening to her jabber away about her garden or cats or the latest scuttlebutt.

Like most of the older houses in Manchester, Mrs. Clarke's had a mail slot in the front door. She would stake out her living-room window each afternoon right about the time I was due, ready to pounce as soon as letters hit hardwood.

Rare was the day I could drop off the mail and keep going. Mrs. C knew she was my last stop, and she was always ready for a little tête-à-tête. She'd lure me into her conversational web with the promise of ice-cold lemonade in the summer and hot cocoa in the colder months. Once Mrs. C got wound up, she could go for a good half hour talking about the trees in her backyard or the family of squirrels that lived in one of them.

She never asked about Rebecca or Megan or Abbey or anything about me, gabbing away like I was there as her personal sounding board. She'd sometimes grow melancholy and talk about how her children and grandchildren hardly ever called.

"And nobody's been to visit me in years," she'd say. "It's like I don't even exist anymore."

I sympathized with her and yet emphasized with them. I could see how she might be a bit trying if you had to take her in larger doses, but she was a good woman, and nobody deserved to be abandoned by family in their old age. She was a kindly, sweet-spirited lady, and it made me a little sad to think that I was likely the highlight of her lonely day.

As I approached her door that Christmas Eve, I knew time was of the essence if I wanted to get Megan's skates before the store closed. Mr. Walker was notoriously prompt. If he said he was closing at six, he'd be closing at six—and not a minute later.

I made a plan as I approached Mrs. Clarke's house. I'd creep up onto the porch, make my drop, and get away before she knew I was there. I cringed when the planks creaked under my boots, but fortunately I remembered she was a bit hard of hearing. I shoved the half-dozen cards and letters into her door slot, lamenting the fact that this nice old lady didn't have more coming her way on Christmas Eve. Where were the packages and gifts, flowers, and chocolates? I heard the mail scatter on her floor and turned to beat a hasty retreat.

"Paul, I thought that was you."

I winced, and turned to see Mrs. Clarke peering out through the screen. "Won't you come in for a cup of hot cider? I've made fresh-baked Christmas cookies."

I didn't want to disappoint this kindly old lady—especially on Christmas Eve. I knew she'd probably been waiting all afternoon for me to show up and had baked those cookies and brewed that cider in anticipation of my arrival. I hesitated. *Maybe Megan doesn't need another gift.* After all, there were at least half a dozen packages with her name on the tag beneath our tree.

The chimes of Manchester Christian began to peal. Old Walter was ringing in six o'clock. I pictured Megan's eager face as she tore away the wrapping paper the next morning. She'd love those skates. Hal had put them aside for me. I'd given my word I'd be back for them. He'd even knocked ten percent off the price. I imagined Walker turning out the store lights, preparing to head home to his family. He might be lingering a bit to see if I showed up. He'd be annoyed if I stood him up.

"I'm sorry, Mrs. Clarke," I said. "But I'm running a bit late this evening. Perhaps another time." I watched her sag in disappointment.

"I understand," she said quietly. I thought she might play the sympathy card, maybe throw in something about being alone for Christmas, but to her credit, she graciously let me off the hook. "You run along now. I don't want you to be late. And Merry Christmas to you and your family."

"Merry Christmas," I said.

My guilt at turning down Mrs. Clarke's invitation was soon lost in a mad dash to make it to the store before Walker Sporting Goods closed its doors for Christmas. I slipped and nearly took a fall as I rounded the corner and jogged into the square. Hal Walker stood waiting at the front door, his ring of keys dangling from his fingers.

I stumbled up, out of breath, just as the sixth and final chime pealed, and the storeowner was turning the key in the front door.

"Hal! Wait!" Walker turned to me and smiled.

"Another minute later, Bennett, and you woulda missed me. Skates you wanted, right?"

"That's right," I said. "The pair in the window."

CHAPTER THIRTEEN

Christmas morning started out as it usually did, with Megan and Abbey springing from their beds at the first glimmer of light. Together, they raced down the upstairs hallway to Mommy and Daddy's room and launched an all-out attack.

"Let's open the presents! Let's open the presents!" The Bennett girls chanted the singsong mantra as they bounced up and down on our bed. There would be no negotiating, no pleas for more sleep. Rebecca and I knew from Christmases past it was best to surrender to their demands.

We were a young family, yet already steeped in our Bennett Christmas ritual. Christmas Eve, we'd dine on Becca's homemade chili and cornbread (a culinary tradition handed down from Becca's paternal grandfather) and then bundle up and stroll the four short blocks to Manchester Christian for Pastor Joe's traditional, yet always somehow surprising, sermon. Each year, he managed to put a fresh spin on the story of Bethlehem, Mary, Joseph, and the baby Jesus. Some years he'd focus on joy and hope, and others he'd accent love or peace. This particular year, light and the Christmas star were at the center of his oration.

"*And having heard the king, they went their way; and lo, the star, which they had seen in the east, went on before them, until it came and stood over where the child was. And when they saw the star, they rejoiced with exceeding great joy.*'

"The star of old was a beacon," our minister said, "that still shines today in the hearts of those who believe in the eternal promise and glory of that night. The Bethlehem babe was a light unto the world that can never be extinguished."

The church choir was particularly rousing that night. The time-honored Christmas songs resounded through the sanctuary, and I imagined the voices drifting out beyond the church, rising higher and higher into the Christmas Eve night sky. As we sang along to "Joy to the World," I looked at my girls. They were singing out loud, glowing in the inspiration of the moment. Rebecca saw me watching her and leaned over and whispered in my ear.

"It doesn't get much better than this, does it?"

I just smiled and nodded. I knew she was right.

After the sermon, we'd usually join one of the groups of carolers who'd form up in the church foyer and then fan out in the surrounding neighborhoods in choirs of six and eight. While I was more inclined to head home after the service, Meg and Abbey always insisted that we go along. Rebecca weighed in on their side. I think she loved the caroling as much as the girls did.

"C'mon," she'd say to me when she saw me waffling. "It's only once a year."

Our Christmas Eve festivities concluded with the girls in their PJs, curled up by the fireplace in the den. I would plunk down in my favorite leather chair and read to them from an old weathered hardback copy of *The Night Before Christmas*. I read slowly and painstakingly, pausing to display the artwork on each page. Invariably, little Abbey would be asleep by the time I reached "bowlful of jelly." Then, I'd gently swing her onto my shoulders and carry her upstairs while Megan tagged along behind, hanging onto the back of my shirt. Becca would join me in their room, and we'd tuck them in together. Then, we'd rendezvous in the kitchen for a midnight mug of cocoa and drink a toast to the miracle of Christmas.

A half hour after the girls began their Christmas morning assault on brightly colored packages that bore their names, there was one lone gift left untouched beneath the tree, and Abbey was holding it.

"Meggy, this one has your name on it. Says it's from Santa."

She handed the clumsily wrapped red-and-green package to her big sis. Rebecca looked at me and whispered.

"You should have let me wrap it."

I smiled and took a sip of peppermint cocoa. Of course, she was right. However, despite my haphazard wrapping job, Megan was respectful and took her time, meticulously folding back the Christmas-tree paper with great care as if she might hurt its feelings. Our oldest daughter loved the drama of the opening almost as much as the gift inside.

"Oh!" she gasped when the contents were revealed. She put her hand to her mouth, and I smiled at her unfeigned amazement.

"Wow," Abbey said when she saw her sister's gift. "Skates!"

Megan held up her new-old leather ice skates like she'd unwrapped a Fabergé egg. She looked right at me. Somehow, she knew I was her St. Nick. She jumped in my lap and threw her arms around my neck.

"Thank you! Thank you! Thank you!"

"Why are you thanking Daddy?" Abbey said. "Card said 'From Santa.'"

Megan smiled at her kid sister. "Because I know Daddy told Santa to get them for me."

The moment she had her new skates in hand, Megan was champing at the bit to try them out.

"Please! I'll be careful! I promise!" Megan knew how to wear her father down. She only had to look into my face with those woefully pleading sea-green eyes. "The other kids are all going skating. Please, Dad! Please, Mom!"

"Honey, it's Christmas," Rebecca said. "It's family time."

Feeling some mild resistance from her mother, Megan focused her lobbying on me. "Please! I'll just go for a little while."

I initially backed up my wife, which would send Megan back to her mother to try to soften her resolve. Our oldest daughter was persistent and unrelenting, and I figured those traits would serve her well later in life. Once she elicited a "Whatever your father thinks" from her mother, I knew it was all over. Megan would turn her full gaze on me, and there was no further point in going through the motions.

"You'll stay near the shore?" I said.

"Yes! I just want to try them out a little, and then I'll come right home."

I looked back at Rebecca to get her final okay, but she was busy with the wrapping-paper cleanup. I took my time, as if I were actually considering denying her request, or at least adding on some meaningless caveat. In fact, I just wanted her to work a little harder.

"Please," Megan said again. "I just want to break them in. Then I'll clean my room and help cook Christmas dinner." The room-cleanup offer told me my eldest daughter was truly desperate to strap on those skates. I finally breathed a laborious sigh, as if I were no longer able to stand up to her withering plea-bargaining.

"All right," I said. "But if you don't dress warmly enough, I'll make you do it again."

"Yes!" Megan said. She kissed me on both cheeks and ran upstairs to get dressed. I walked to the living-room window. It was a clear blue Christmas Day and still cold enough that the icicles weren't dripping. *The pond's been frozen solid for over a month,* I figured. Everything will be all right.

"I wanna go, too," Abbey said. Rebecca could tell by the look I tossed her way that I didn't like the idea. I knew that if Abbey went I'd have to go as well, and I had things to do around the house.

"But I need you to stay and help me bake Christmas cookies," Rebecca said, shooting me a furtive smile. Abbey frowned and crossed her arms defiantly. "I'll let you put the sprinkles on." The little girl smiled. Mom had sold her.

"Sure you don't want to come, Daddy?" A few minutes later, I stood in the backyard and inspected my firstborn. She was wearing her neon-pink winter coat and lavender ski hat. My old ratty maroon wool scarf—the same scarf Rebecca had brought back to me that night in Brooklyn—was tucked inside her collar. She held up her hands to show me that her brown knit mittens were in place. She had her Christmas skates slung over her shoulder.

"You're a big girl," I said. "I trust you. Besides, Mommy's got me on light-replacement detail."

"Sounds fun," Megan said with a smile. "Daddy, I really like my skates."

"I'm glad," I said. "I made 'em myself."

Megan smiled. "You did not." I winked at her.

"Half hour," I said. "One good turn around the pond and then you come home."

"Okay, Daddy." Then she gave me a quick kiss on the cheek, and I watched my beloved Meggy jog off through the crunchy snow toward Waller's Pond.

I called after her.

"Megan, you watch the ice. Be smart."

"I will, Daddy! I love you."

In the years ahead, I would look back on that moment and replay again and again Megan's parting.

I love you.

Those were the last earthly words I would ever hear her speak, but instead of that bringing me some measure of comfort, the echo of that sweet sentiment became a dagger to my heart, a sharp thrust of pain and guilt. My Megan had loved me, and I'd failed her. I should have gone along; I should have dragged my own skates out of mothballs and joined her on the ice. I should have been there to watch her steps and hold her hand, to keep her from harm.

But as I watched her cut through the woods that Christmas morning, I could hear the laughter and shouts from the other children already out on Waller's Pond. *She'll be okay,* I told myself. *Let her have some fun.*

With Megan off skating and Rebecca baking cookies with Abbey, I replaced some burned-out Christmas lights. Even though I knew they'd only be up another week, I also knew if I didn't take care of it, I'd hear about it from my perfectionist wife. She'd already dropped a few none-too-subtle hints.

"Honey, I think I noticed a bulb or two burned out in the front yard."

"I'm on it, babe," I said and then put it off as long as possible.

As I went about the job of locating the dead bulbs, the joyful sounds drifted from Waller's Pond. How lucky these small-town kids were, I thought. If you wanted to ice-skate in New York, you had to wait in line and then, once your turn finally arrived, jostle and joust for precious ice space. They had a big old pond, all the time in the world, and plenty of room to move around.

"Help!"

The voice was high-pitched, greatly distressed, and coming from the pond. I couldn't tell if it was a boy or a girl. I hesitated, as if I wasn't quite sure what I'd heard. I stood there by the fence, stupidly clutching a strand of lights in my left hand.

"Help!"

The second cry was louder, more desperate. The pond was only about a hundred and fifty yards straight through the woods that bordered the backyards along Bethlehem Place.

I hit the tree line at a full-on sprint, plunging through icy foot-deep snow, dodging trees and stumps and fallen branches, staggering and stumbling in a desperate race through the leafless forest.

"Help. Please! Somebody!"

My mad dash took less than a minute, but it seemed endless, like I was running in a dream where, just as I neared my destination, it moved away from me. I could only think of Megan and her pink jacket and purple ski beanie. If one of her friends had fallen through the ice, she'd be right there trying to help. *Don't do anything stupid, Meggy. Wait for Daddy.*

As I broke out of the woods at the edge of the pond, a terrible dread gripped me and sucked the air from my chest.

I couldn't see pink.

Where was Megan's bright-pink coat? Then I saw a cluster of kids standing at the edge of the pond. A red-faced boy saw me and pointed out across the ice. What was he pointing at? There was nothing there. Then I saw them, the jagged fissures aiming to a hole about twenty yards from where I was standing. Resting on the ice next to the hole . . . was my old maroon scarf.

CHAPTER FOURTEEN

"There is nothing I can say today to comfort those who loved Megan."

The mourners at Megan's funeral filled the pews and spilled out into the foyer of Manchester Christian. It was three days after she'd fallen through the ice and drowned at Waller's Pond, and almost the entire town was there to pay tribute. There were our neighbors and friends, fellow churchgoers, and practically all of my postal customers. Even Mrs. Clarke was there, though it must have been some challenge for her to make her way through the icy streets.

Pastor Joe's vibrancy and youthful glow was missing that day. He was pale and gaunt, and the dark circles under his eyes said he hadn't slept in days. His wife, Erin, sat next to Rebecca on the front pew, holding my wife's hand. The preacher's young wife had red eyes and puffy cheeks. She was barely holding it together.

As he delivered his halting eulogy, the young minister had none of the eloquence and polish we'd all grown so accustomed to. That morning, Joe Moody's storytelling skills had abandoned him. Sitting in the front row between Rebecca and Abbey, I stared straight ahead, refusing to meet the pastor's eye. My jaw was set, my hands clenched and tense.

In the three days since Megan's death, I'd lost the ability to think clearly, living on some sort of strange autopilot that enabled me to move and breathe and eat and function involuntarily. It was as if my body had its own separate operating system running on a generator that had kicked in when the power went off. I had seen things in those seventy-two hours that seemed to be torn right out of the pages of somebody else's nightmare. I'd stood by staring blankly as the paramedics lifted my baby's cold, waterlogged body from the icy lake. I'd watched as the coroner's wagon drove her away to the morgue. The last thing I glimpsed was a snatch of pink as they slammed shut those dreadful doors.

I'd held my sobbing wife in my arms as she collapsed with the news and locked eyes with Abbey as she watched us wide-eyed and wondering what terrible thing could make her mommy cry like that. Rebecca and I had come together in a moment of heroism; we had saved a stranger from the lake that summer day, but we weren't there to save our own child. A witness said Meg had been laughing, waving to a friend on the shore when the cracking sound came. And then she vanished.

"I'm sorry, Mr. Bennett, but I'm afraid she's gone."

From the moment the paramedic uttered those terrible words, I knew that my relationship with any so-called God, if there were such a being at all, was over.

I listened time and again as well-meaning friends and neighbors offered lines of comfort that were anything but comforting.

"It's God's will."

"She's in a much better place."

"The Lord has called her home."

I would accept them without comment and quickly move away before I could say something I would later regret. All my churchgoing and gratitude-giving and praying and praising had all been for nothing. The one time I'd really needed him, he'd let me down. God hadn't been there.

I concluded I'd been wasting my time going to church and sitting in that pew and listening to Pastor Joe talk about goodness and love and faith. And then it became clear that maybe my first instincts were right. There was no God at all. And even if there were, he took my sweet girl from me, so I wanted no part of him. Not anymore. Not ever.

◆ ◆ ◆

I changed in a moment that Christmas Day. I began the day as one Paul Thomas Bennett and ended it as a man I barely recognized. Gone were my innocence and my hopes for the future—my dreams. And all I wanted to do was disappear. My thoughts tormented me day and night and filled my head with recurring nightmares that played over and over like a skipping record. There was Megan walking away from me, calling out "I love you." There were those dreaded cries for help and that frayed scarf lying on the ice near the hole that took my little girl.

Abbey changed, too. Our outgoing and fun-loving five-year-old, from the moment she learned her big sister was gone, clammed up and wouldn't utter another syllable. It was as if the sounds that had spilled so freely from her lips from the moment she was born just ran out—she'd used up her quota of words and had no more to give and no desire to give them.

"I've heard of this," Rebecca said. "It's called traumatic mutism. It happened to me once, when I was a girl."

Rebecca first told me the story at summer camp during one of our sunset walks along the lake. She was a year younger than Abbey when her grandmother Mimi came to visit from Florida. Little Rebecca was in the living room one evening playing with her nanny when her mother asked her to go call Mimi to dinner.

"My mother said, 'Rebecca, darling, go tell Mimi it's time to eat.' I remember having this strange sense of foreboding as I moved down the long hallway toward my grandmother's room. I somehow knew what I was going to find."

When young Rebecca didn't find her grandmother in the guest room, she walked into the bathroom. "Mimi was dead in the bathtub," Rebecca said. "Her eyes were fixed and sightless, like in the movies. It was such a shock, and I was so traumatized I didn't utter a word for nearly two days after. It felt a little like having the breath knocked out of me, and I'd forgotten how to form words. When I finally spoke, the first thing I said was 'Mimi's in the bathtub.' My words were on a delay, and I went right back to the moment I saw her there."

Abbey's condition was worse. Far worse. At first, we expected that her problem would simply work itself out, but when a week passed and she still hadn't spoken, Rebecca made an appointment to see our pediatrician, Dr. Baker. When she told me she'd done this, I snapped at her.

"What's a doctor going to do? Bring her sister back?" I instantly wanted to snatch back the words. How could I say such a thing? The pain had broken my ability to censor myself.

In the end, I refused to go with her. I thought it was a waste of time, and apparently, I was right. Doc Baker told Rebecca there was little to be done.

"Her voice will come back," he said. "It just may take some time."

But, our little girl's words didn't come back. As the days and weeks passed and Abbey remained closed off in her world of silence, I began to wonder if she'd ever speak again. A part of me was afraid of what she'd say if she did start talking. Would she blame me for what happened? I knew *I* blamed me, and I was pretty sure Rebecca blamed me, so why shouldn't she? After all, it was my fault. I'd bought the skates. I'd let her go alone. I didn't get there in time. I loathed the day I saw those skates in the window of Walker Sporting Goods. I loathed the lights and decorations and carols and symbols of the stupid, pointless overlong season that had conspired to take our beautiful daughter from us. I hated Christmas, and if I'd had the power, I would have swept it from the face of the earth.

I was given three weeks' bereavement leave from the Manchester Post Office, and I didn't know what to do with them. I found myself moping around the house, trying to keep busy, wallowing in guilt so intense I sometimes couldn't get my breath. Sleep came in fits and starts, and I dreaded it when it did come, though the few dreams that weren't filled with horror and death were the only relief I had from the torture of my every waking moment. For in those rare, fleeting dreams, I could live in a world where the pain and sorrow couldn't find me. Those dreams became my drug, a nonsensical temporary escape from the mind-numbing dread and dull ache that had settled on my brain like an ocean fog. I became immune to everything but my own suffering, so wrapped up in my misery I paid little attention to my wife's pain. I had no comfort to give, no solace or sympathy. My guilt had consumed me body and soul.

I started taking long, aimless walks after supper. People would see me and call out greetings, but I'd ignore them. I'd keep my eyes straight ahead, my hands shoved down deep in my coat pockets, acting as if I didn't hear them at all. My natural friendliness had vanished. I kept my eyes down, my gaze fixed at my feet.

One evening, I altered my route to take me by the ABC Liquor Store on Jackson Street. I'd never set foot in there. To me, liquor stores had always seemed seedy and unseemly. My father didn't drink; Rebecca only had wine on special occasions, and I'd never really acquired the taste for alcohol. Not going to college surely helped.

The first time by I slowed my pace as I passed, looking over at the store like a shy high school kid trying to get the courage to ask his crush to the dance. I pondered my tortured thoughts, wondering if I could find an escape in that little store with the dirty windows and flickering neon sign. Was it even possible to find relief? The next evening I stopped, thought about going in, and forced myself to keep moving. I knew that if I walked through that door, I might never come out. The third night I again forced myself to keep walking but then stopped at the corner, looking back at the pink neon.

I'll just go in and look around, I told myself. *Won't buy anything. What could that hurt?*

I bought a bottle of cheap whiskey that first time. It was an evening in late March. Megan had been gone three months to the day.

From then on, it became my daily routine. After a day's work, I'd head home for supper and then head out unannounced on my evening walks that turned into night walks. Before I knew it, those walks lasted into the wee hours of the next morning. My first stop was always the liquor store. Eventually, I stopped going home altogether. I'd finish my postal rounds, change into my street clothes at the post office, and head straight to the ABC Store.

I'd vary my drink of choice from day to day. Beer. A fifth of scotch. Whiskey. My final destination was always the same. I'd take my brown-bagged bottle and head out to Waller's Pond, where I'd plunk down on the rickety wooden bench at the end of the old creaky dock. I'd turn up my crumpled bag like a practiced wino and stare out across the water.

That terrible Christmas morning would play over and over on a loop in my mind. Sometimes, I'd see myself reaching out and grasping for Megan's desperate fingers, but in my vision, they were always just out of reach. She would stare at me, wide-eyed and horrified, wondering why I couldn't help her, why I couldn't save her. Other times, I'd grab her hand an instant before it sunk beneath the surface and pull her out and into my arms—but the ice beneath us would crack with our collective weight, and we'd both go down together, sinking deep into some cold and endless abyss. I preferred the latter nightmares to the former.

I'd stagger home sometime after two in the morning and pass out on the living-room couch. And there, the worst dreams of all would come: Megan staring up at me from beneath the ice, lips moving, mouthing desperate words I could never quite make out. In those dreams, I would punch and pound on the ice until my knuckles bled, desperately trying to get to her. But no matter what I did, no matter how hard I hit that ice—it just wouldn't give.

CHAPTER FIFTEEN

Before the accident on Waller's Pond, Rebecca and I believed our marriage was unshakable. We thought our relationship was somehow stronger because of the heroic feat we'd shared that afternoon in the rainstorm. We'd persevered despite her parents' best efforts to derail our budding romance. We'd overcome our class differences, defied the odds of youth and inexperience, and found that our love had thrived despite all the arguments against its survival. We thought our union was invincible.

But in those dark days after Megan died, we discovered we'd been naïve. Few marriages are strong enough to survive the loss of a child, and we came to realize, that terrible winter and spring, that ours was the rule rather than the exception. Of course, we had no way of knowing it, but our love story was doomed from the moment Megan walked out of the yard that Christmas morning. It was over as soon as I spotted those old skates in the display window of Walker Sporting Goods, as soon as I offered a rain check for Mrs. Clarke's fresh-baked cookies, as soon as I decided that light-bulb replacement took precedence over spending time with my daughter. Our marriage didn't end the day Megan fell through the ice, but it was mortally wounded that Christmas morning. Our marital death would be slow and painful, our once unshakable love would gradually bleed out, and as I watched our demise grow closer and closer, I found I had no desire to stanch the bleeding. Despite Rebecca's best efforts to keep our family intact, over time my pain and weakness and guilt would seal the Bennett family's fate.

Yes, Rebecca did everything she could to keep us from floundering. She seemed determined to pull me out of my drunken spiral and liberate me from my cocoon of guilt and pain. I watched her desperate efforts to save us and resolved to fight her every step of the way. Though I wouldn't have admitted this at the time, I was afraid that if she succeeded—if I was able to resume some semblance of a normal life—it would absolve me from what had happened. I didn't deserve absolution or a return to normalcy. I didn't deserve even a moment of peace for what I had let happen. I didn't deserve Rebecca or Abbey or our home. To me, moving on in any way, shape, or form would be diminishing Megan's loss. It was only later that I came to realize it wasn't her memory I was desperate to keep alive—it was her death, and the blame I placed squarely on my own shoulders. I was the one who bought those skates. It was me.

Rebecca watched the old Paul slowly drain away until she no longer recognized the shell of a man that shared her roof. It was as if the fun-loving, outgoing Paul had been exorcised and his body claimed by a bitter counterpart. I no longer even looked the same. The lightness of being that had once radiated off me was drained away until my face and gaze and essence had hardened into something older and gaunt, and my eyes seemed darker and cold. But Rebecca, being Rebecca, wasn't about to lose me without putting up a fight. And instead of appreciating her loyalty, I did everything I could to push her to that breaking point, to force her hand.

On at least a half-dozen occasions, Rebecca set up marital counseling sessions with Pastor Joe, and each time I promised I'd be there. I never showed. I would intend on going, would even make my way toward the church, but I never made it. I'd always turn back, end up at the ABC Store, and then out at the lake, bottle clutched firmly in hand. When Rebecca would confront me later, I'd just shrug.

"I was busy."

"Paul, we need to talk about this," she'd say. "We need to try and save our marriage."

I'd always walk away without answering. I no longer believed in what the good pastor was preaching. The bottle was my counselor, my minister, my shrink, and my best friend. The bottle was the only god I needed.

Becca continued her tirelessly relentless efforts to cling to our marriage. Time and again, she tried to reach out to me. She was tender and kind and hopeful that I would come back—that the Paul she'd so long loved would return to her. Through my cold indifference and drunken stupors and unavailability, I tried to let her know that the old Paul was dead and gone, but she wouldn't quit. For a long time, her faith in our marriage—her faith in me—refused to waver. She simply wouldn't let go. But I was soon to learn, even Rebecca Anne Waverly, the patient and tolerant and hopeful, had her limits.

One night, I overheard Rebecca as I lay in the backyard hammock drinking a beer. It was summer, and Megan had been gone some two and a half years. I was slightly buzzed, staring up at the stars, my mind dull and dead and unfocused. A typical evening. Becca was up in Abbey's room, tucking her in, and the window was open. Abbey was going on eight years old, and we'd long grown used to the fact that she no longer used words to communicate. In all other respects, she seemed to be a happy, well-adjusted little girl. She played and smiled and hugged and went to school and had friends. She just didn't speak.

"Tonight, we're gonna pray for Daddy. Okay?" I heard Becca say.

I could picture little Abbey climbing out of bed and taking a spot beside her mommy on the floor, hands clasped, eyes clenched, following her lead. It had been so long since I'd heard my little girl's voice that I'd nearly forgotten what she sounded like. I wondered if she'd grow up and spend her whole life in silence. Would she be able to meet some-one—fall in love and start a family—if she never spoke?

"Dear God," Rebecca prayed. "We know you're up there, and that you're watching over us. We have a favor to ask you. Will you please look after Daddy? We love him very much, and we know you do, too. Tonight, we'd like to ask that you please give him a little extra love and care. Thank you for listening, God. Amen."

I tried to feel something when I heard my wife's humble prayer. I knew that feeling was probably a good thing. *If only I could break down and cry,* I thought as I swayed in the hammock, my right foot dragging on the ground. *If only I could let it all out.*

If only.

I finished my beer and let the bottle slip from my fingers and drop with a thud to the grass. I stared up at the clear night sky; the stars I once looked on with awe and wonder now seemed like dead lights. Sometime after midnight, I finally drifted off to sleep.

Rebecca took a far different path after we lost Megan. Despite her own tortured grief and pain, she wouldn't let the nightmare of that Christmas Day destroy her. Hours after her daughter was taken from her, she was orchestrating the funeral and making arrangements. When I refused to go to the cemetery with her to pick out a plot, she asked Erin Moody to go.

Becca picked out the headstone, decided on the inscription, and worked with Megan's principal to plant a sugar maple in her memory on school grounds. And she did it all without my help or support. I wasn't there to hold her hand or offer words of comfort. I was as absent as if I'd packed up and moved to Alaska.

I should have been impressed with my wife for stepping up and being the strong one in a time of crisis. Instead, I wanted Rebecca to hold God accountable for letting our little girl die. I wanted her to hate, too.

Instead, Rebecca began to pray more often, kept up the nightly gratitude-game ritual with Abbey, and didn't miss a Sunday service. She was even in church the Sunday after Megan's funeral when I was in the bathroom throwing up and hoping for a heart attack or a brain hemorrhage or anything that would quickly and suddenly put me out of my grief-stricken misery.

Becca threw herself even more wholeheartedly into church life. She volunteered for extra outreach work, signed on to teach Sunday school, and even served on the bereavement committee saying, "I think I'm uniquely qualified."

I confronted her late one summer night when I stumbled through the door. I'd been at Waller's Pond again. I was drunk . . . again . . . and spoiling for a fight.

"How can you still go to church? How can you still believe in God?" I asked. My words tumbled out in a half slur, half hiss.

Rebecca kept her cool. "In order for me to go on with my life," she said, "I have to believe that Megan's still being cared for—that God has taken up where we left off. I have to believe she's okay, and so I do believe."

Dizzy and disoriented, I glared at her. "*Okay?*" I said. "You have to believe she's okay? She's dead, Becca. Gone. She no longer exists. I killed her. I got her those skates. It's on me. If there were a God, don't you think he would have stopped me? If there were a God, I never would have seen those skates or they never would have been there in the first place. If there's a God, either he doesn't care or he let this happen. He let Megan die. He let me get those skates."

"I don't blame you, Paul, if that's what you're afraid of," Rebecca said. "I never blamed you, and I never will."

Those words should have given me solace, but instead self-loathing welled up within me, so I hurled it right back at her. "You believe whatever fool thing you want to. I'm going to be a realist from now on. No more believing in fantasies or magical fairies in the sky. I used to respect you, Becca," I said. "I used to think you were so smart. Now, I just pity you." I waved a dismissive hand at her as if she wasn't even worth my time. "I'm going to sleep out in the shed."

I was surprised to feel a twinge of regret as I stumbled out into the dark to my little hideaway that night. Was there a flicker of humanity left in me? My words had been intended to hurt, and from the look on my wife's face, I'd found my mark. I hesitated at the shed door, leaning on the wall to catch my balance, and considered going back inside. *Maybe I should even apologize.* I looked back at the house and considered trying to make things right, and then my dark and vicious thoughts came back in full force. An apology would be hollow, for I had meant every wrathful and disillusioned word.

From that night on I never slept in the house again. Most nights, I'd go straight from my alcohol-fueled ramblings out back to my lair and crash for the night. I avoided my wife and daughter, acting like a tenant rather than a father. I cut myself off from my family until they didn't even feel like family anymore. After Becca caught on to my routine, she made sure to have supper waiting for me on a plate warmer in the shed. Sometimes I'd eat it, other times I'd be so wasted from alcohol I'd hurl the plate out in the backyard. Then I'd pass out.

During the time of my nightly pity benders, I somehow managed to keep my job at the post office. I learned to be a skillful compartmentalizer. It wasn't difficult to deliver the mail with a raging hangover. Each morning at ten, I'd simply pick up my daily sack, avoiding any contact with Postmaster Ray or anybody else at the post office, and head out on my rounds, shuffling along like a zombie, delivering the mail on emotionless autopilot.

But Manchester was, after all, a small town, and news of my daily drunken ritual eventually trickled back to my boss. One morning, Postmaster Ray cornered me as I was about to head out on my rounds.

"Bennett. Could I see you in my office, please?"

I offered up a fainthearted lie. "Ray, can we do this another time? I've got to knock off early today. Abbey's got a doctor's appointment."

"It'll just take a minute," he said. I sighed loudly enough for him to hear, dropped my sack, walked into his office, and plunked down in the chair across from his desk. I was halfway off the edge of the chair, signaling that I expected a short conversation. My throbbing head was in a particularly ornery mood that morning. Ray was curt and to the point.

"Paul, you're a drunk, and if you keep going down the path you're on, you will no longer be an employee of the Manchester Post Office."

I glared at him. "Anything else?"

Ray leaned back in his chair, folding his hands behind his bald head. "The way you're acting—getting drunk and staying out all night—all you're doing is disgracing Megan's memory."

I felt the veins bulge in my neck. He'd overstepped, mentioning Megan. I could feel my teeth grinding, my jaw clenching up. If his expression was any indication, he knew he'd struck a chord, and he didn't care.

"We done here?" I asked.

"Yeah," he said.

I was still fuming as I headed out on my rounds. Who did that jerk think he was? Nobody had a right to speak to me that way. I was a grieving father. He had no idea. Who was Ray Waldrop to judge me? I wanted to turn around, go back in that office, and hurl my sack of letters at him. I wanted to tell him what he could do with this stupid, mindless, soul-sucking job.

He'd accused me of being a disgrace to Megan's memory. How dare he? I had a right to be angry, a right to my rage. It was mine. Sometimes I felt as if it was all I had left. But as I walked my rounds that morning, my hangover pounding inside my head, I came to realize that Ray, the cue-ball postmaster, was right. I was a pathetic, wallowing drunk, and my life was barreling down a steep grade like a locomotive with no brakes. The crash was not going to be pretty. Whether I deserved them or not, I still had a family, and even in my pitiable state, they needed me. My Abbey deserved a Daddy.

So I made an effort to get it together and clean up my act. I knew I couldn't handle cold turkey so, little by little, I began to cut down on the weeknight drinking, the long late-night walks, and the trips to Waller's Pond. And thus began a gradual return to normalcy. I went from seven drunken nights a week to five and then three until I finally managed to get through an entire week without so much as a sip of alcohol. When I ran into him in the grocery store, the ABC storeowner even commented on it.

"Haven't seen you around much lately. Not sure how I should feel about that."

I started showing up home at a respectable hour. Sometimes, I'd even make it in time for dinner. Occasionally, I'd bring Abbey a toy or Rebecca a few flowers from Linder's Florist on the town square. I was like an actor reprising an old well-known part. *Paul Bennett returns to the stage in the role of dependable husband and doting father.* But the joy was gone. I knew, even as I went through the motions, that I couldn't keep it up forever. Pretending to be normal again was never really going to work.

And I could feel Rebecca's cautious optimism at her husband's apparent turnaround. Though I was still sleeping in the shed out back, she seemed grateful at my ostensible rebirth. Maybe she believed her prayers had worked—maybe she truly thought I was coming back to them. Maybe we could have some kind of marriage again. Maybe there could be life after Megan. But as the weeks rolled into months and then to years, Becca came to sense what I knew deep in my heart—my about-face wasn't real, and it wouldn't last long. Even after I stopped my alcoholic binges, Rebecca and I were still cool and somewhat distant. The spark was gone, the affection missing. Whether we knew it or not at the time, the love story of Rebecca and Paul had entered its final act.

"Can't we at least put lights on the fence this year?" Rebecca said. "How about a wreath on the door? For Abbey's sake." It was the year of my apparent resurgence, and Becca decided she'd push for a little more Christmas. The year after Megan's accident I had put a moratorium on Christmas decorations at 25 Bethlehem Place. I told Rebecca that if she tried to put any up, I'd tear them down. I told her that I hated Christmas and wanted no part in its celebration. If it had been up to me, I would have eliminated the holiday altogether.

The moment Thanksgiving was over, I slipped into a fog of despair. It was during those dreaded days of December when I felt the bottle pulling at me like a magnet, and I became even more withdrawn and morose. For Abbey's sake, I agreed to a simple tree and three stockings on the mantel—that was it. Rebecca well knew my feelings on the subject, but as the years passed and December rolled into December, she'd still lobby me for a little more, thinking I'd soften my opposition.

I may have held Christmas partially responsible for Megan's death, but Abbey sure didn't. Each year, when December rolled around, she'd tug on her mother's arm and guide her to the closet where we kept the art supplies. Our refrigerator would soon be filled with drawings of snowmen, reindeer, and jolly ol' St. Nicks. Abbey seemed to know that her daddy didn't care much for the holiday but also that—if she made the decorations herself—he was powerless to protest. When Rebecca figured this out, she encouraged the budding little artist to have at it, keeping her supplied with glue; red and green construction paper; and silver, red, and gold glitter.

Then, as the fourth Christmas since we'd lost Megan approached, something happened that shattered our uneasy truce, something that knocked me violently off the wagon.

I had decided to pass a lazy Saturday in late November cleaning out the old writer's shed. I hadn't given it a good scrubbing since I'd started sleeping there. Becca had offered to do the job herself at least a dozen times, but I'd put her off. I liked the clutter. It made it seem somehow less empty. Finally, the smell of rotting food, the strange bugs, and the fog of dust forced me to take action.

With a couple of large plastic trash bags in hand, I set about the grimy work, leaving my desk for last. As I bent down to take a gander underneath, I found a half-dozen stray papers clustered among the cobwebs and dead flies. I scooped them out with one sweep of my hand, revealing a sheet of yellowed typing paper. I picked it up, blew off the dust, and stared down at it. At the top of the page was typed . . . *one misspelled word*. I knew in a moment what it was. It was Megan's first word.

"Dadddy."

I sat on the floor and held it up in the light. In a flash, I was back in that moment—a summer evening—the first time Meg had toddled out to the shed and crawled up in my lap. She wasn't even three years old yet. I could see us there in the golden twilight. I could hear her little voice, her giggle and sweet laugh as I guided her tiny fingers across the typewriter keys, helping her press down hard.

"I'm typing!" she'd said, her tone full of wonder. "I wanna spell 'Daddy.'"

Of course, I was flattered that I'd been deemed worthy of her first typed word. I helped her find the letters and watched as she carefully and firmly punched the keys.

When she finished, she yanked the paper out of the carriage and proudly handed it to me as a keepsake. I promised to cherish it, but somewhere along the way, a gust of wind had blown through the window and scattered my clutter of papers to the floor, where they remained hidden and discarded until the day of my cleaning.

I sat there holding that memento, and felt Megan with me again. I could see her red curls, feel her chubby arms around my neck, and hear that little laugh rising up from some distant other side where I hoped against hope and agnostic doubt that she still played and enjoyed—and loved.

It was all simply too much. Four years had passed. Megan would have been thirteen. A teenager. She would have been talking about boys and putting on makeup and growing tall and pretty, and it would have been something to see: our little girl growing up. I would have gone to her soccer games and ballet recitals and helped her with her English papers and gone on long autumn walks, and we would have chased falling leaves and kept score to see who caught the most. I would have teased her about the latest boy she liked and pointed out his many faults and why he in no way deserved a girl like her. We would have been good friends.

I sat for a moment, staring at the paper in my hand, and then I folded it carefully, tucked it in my shirt pocket, and walked out.

◆ ◆ ◆

The next morning, Reggie, a beat cop from Manchester PD, found me passed out on the dock at Waller's Pond. I was clutching an empty vodka bottle, and I had soiled myself. He brought me home and, with Rebecca's help, took me inside the house, where they gently placed me on the couch, and there I stayed for two days until I woke up late one night to find Abbey standing over me. I was curled up in a ball in front of the fireplace. She was looking down at me, her little lavender security blanket clutched in her right hand. There were tears streaming down her rosy cheeks. She was pointing behind me, her face a mixture of heartbreak and fear. I rolled over and looked at what she was staring at. Our three family stockings had been ripped down from the mantel, and all that was left of them were charred crusts of black ash fabric, smoldering in the fire. I could just make out the A and the Y on Abbey's blackened stocking. Our modest tree was toppled over, the ornaments shattered, the lights in a tangle. I knew I'd done it—I had to have done it—but I had no memory of the act. I'd been drunk and delusional and out of my head, but I'd been the culprit, and there was my little girl as a silent witness to my debauchery. Another low point on my downward spiral. Maybe the lowest.

I tried to sit up, tried to reach out to her, but she took a step back. She was afraid of me. My precious angel was afraid of Daddy. And then it hit me with such searing clarity. I'd let her down; I'd let both my daughters down. Abbey no longer spoke, and that was my fault, too. Our eyes met, and the sadness and loss there was so deep, deeper than mine. And I wondered whom she blamed for her sister being gone. Did she blame Santa for bringing the skates? And if she did, would that blame shift to me . . . as soon as she found out the truth?

And then Rebecca was there. I hadn't heard her come down the stairs. She tied her robe around her and looked from Abbey to me to the living-room disaster I'd wrought. The look she gave me, as she took Abbey in her arms, said she was finished. My Becca had given up on me. And it only stood to reason, for I'd given up on me long before.

Rebecca called Ray at the post office and said I had laryngitis. She hated to lie but felt she had no choice. She knew if I lost my job it'd be all over. I'd have nothing left, no reason to get out of bed in the morning except to scrounge my next drink. Maybe it was having to lie for me that finally pushed her over the edge. Maybe it was the way I had looked and smelled when the cop brought me home that morning. Whatever it was, Rebecca decided enough was enough.

"Paul. We need to talk."

It was the night of December 12, and I was sagging at the kitchen table hunched over a cup of black coffee, nursing yet another hangover. Becca'd just tucked Abbey in. She came in and sat across from me.

We need to talk. Rebecca had once told me that good news never followed those four words. As Becca looked at me, tears welled up in her eyes. I knew what was coming.

"Paul, I think we should separate."

CHAPTER SIXTEEN

Rebecca had finally arrived at the inevitable conclusion. Our marriage was over. Christmas Day would mark four years to the day since we lost Megan, and my wife was wise enough to know that things were not going to magically get better. She could sense what I felt, that life on the planet no longer held any joy or hope or motivation. Four years was a long time, and the old Paul was gone and wasn't coming back. She had finally seen the light.

"Did you hear what I said, Paul? I said I think we should separate."

I shrugged as if she'd just asked me what I wanted for dinner. "Sounds right to me," I said. "Isn't that what couples do when they no longer love each other?"

I watched her eyes well up and felt a strange and perverse sense of satisfaction. Yet there was something deep inside me that nearly choked on the words, a part of me that yearned to take them back and was desperate for her to contradict them. Instead, the girl I'd once fallen head over heels for sat across from me and said nothing.

"Told you to go to Yale," I said.

"Paul, don't . . ."

"Your parents were right all along. You made the wrong choice, and now look where it got you: one daughter's dead, the other's mute, and your husband's a raging drunk."

When she looked at me, her eyes seemed somehow older and defeated, as if the last bit of fight had been drained away. She knew I was trying to hurt her and, in the process, shift a little of the blame to her. She didn't bite. I took a different tack. I needed to hurt her, wanted to see her fall apart.

"Why did you marry me anyway? I know why. You wanted to stick it to your parents, right? 'Hey, look Mom, look Dad. I'm marrying a poor boy from Brooklyn.' That's it. Right, Rebecca? I was an act of defiance. Bet you're kicking yourself now, aren't you? Maybe it's not too late. Maybe you can find some rich doctor or lawyer. I'm sure Jane has a few lined up, just waiting for us to fail. You can cry on his shoulder and tell him what a big mistake I was, how you're so happy you have someone like him now."

Rebecca got up from the table. "I'm not doing this, Paul."

"You were the one who wanted to talk," I said. "Guess you want me to make it easy for you."

"No. Not easy," Rebecca said. "But why do you have to make it so hard?"

"It's supposed to be hard," I said. "We're splitting up. Or maybe you want me to 'go gently into that good night.' Sorry. But don't worry, Becca. You can have the house, these things . . . everything. Just promise you'll burn the wedding photos, all the photos, my letters, anything that reminds you I was once a part of your life. I want to be forgotten, Becca. I want to be nothing more than a ghost in your past. A dark memory."

I'd finally done it. I'd landed the knockout punch. I watched the tears curve down her cheeks. My wife. My first love. My Rebecca. Her heart was finally breaking. All her cool and calm composure crumbled right in front of my eyes. But I felt no satisfaction or exhilaration or even a trace of sympathy. I simply felt nothing.

Her voice quivered when she spoke. "How could you think I married you as an act of defiance? I married you because I loved you, Paul. And you loved me."

"That was over a long time ago," I said. My tone was level and emotionless. She looked at me as if expecting me to backpedal. I pressed on. "This is the right decision," I said. "We should have done this four years ago. Right after Megan died."

My words were cold and harsh and unfeeling, and I could see them cut right into her. There was no going back. My words had sealed our fate forever.

All the anger and resentment drained from my body until I was spent and sapped and beaten. I sighed. "What do you want me to do?"

"I think you should move out," Rebecca said. "I don't mean out to the shed. Someplace else." I nodded. "But not until after the holidays. It's going to be hard enough on Abbey as it is." Rebecca stood watching me, as if maybe—just maybe—some faint glimmer of the old Paul might shine through one last time, and then she walked out, leaving me alone with a throbbing ache in my stomach and a cup of cold coffee.

Not long after Rebecca told me she wanted me to move out, she informed me she'd be taking Abbey to New York for Christmas. I came home from work on December 21 to find them already gone. They'd taken a shuttle to the airport. A part of me was glad they were gone. It was easier that way. I wandered into the kitchen and discovered an Abbey-made "Merry Christmas Daddy" card stuck to the fridge that told me to "look under the tree." There was also a sticky note from Rebecca about the meals she'd set aside for me. I wadded up Rebecca's message and tossed it. I would be drinking my supper.

I found a tiny, unevenly wrapped box beneath our sparse Christmas tree. When it came to gift wrapping, Abbey took after her old man. The tag read "To Daddy, Love, Abbey." I peeled it open and lifted out a necklace with a ring on it. It was that cheap Kmart engagement ring I'd given Rebecca at Wollman Rink on that long-ago New Year's Eve.

I'd replaced it with a real diamond not long after I went to work for the post office—my first purchase on my first credit card. Rebecca had put the faux ring away in her jewelry box, where it remained until Abbey found it and had started using the cheap ring and silver chain as a necklace whenever she played dress-up. Mom officially gave it to her on her seventh birthday. Abbey had grinned a mile wide when she opened the little jewelry box and discovered Mommy's ring. And now my little girl was passing it back to me—its original owner. The symbolism seemed perfect. The little fake diamond was a fitting epitaph to an ill-fated romance, to the death of the happily ever after. I tossed the box aside and slipped the necklace in my shirt pocket. It was the best and worst Christmas gift I'd ever received.

◆ ◆ ◆

And so we arrive at my former church on that dark and cold Christmas Eve. Rebecca and Abbey were in New York basking in the glow of a Waverly family Christmas, and I was slogging my way through the icy, empty streets of Manchester trying to get through my rounds before the storm arrived. A bottle of rum waited for me at home. Maybe a bottle of whiskey, too. My Christmas presents to myself. Blizzard or no blizzard, I planned to take my liquid comfort out to that hated pond and get sloshed. If I got lucky, I might just freeze to death.

As the sixth and final peal of the church bell sounded, I thought I glimpsed someone up in the steeple, a flicker of red hair that I knew didn't belong to Walter. I wondered if maybe he was training a bell-ringer apprentice. Could he be retiring after all these years? Unlikely. Walter loved his job so much they'd have to cart him out of that steeple in a body bag.

Must be seeing things. My world-weary mind was playing tricks on me. The old bell fell silent, and it was so quiet on the street I could hear the snowflakes hitting the pavement. A gust of cold wind kicked up a wisp of snow. Then, I heard it. However, I wasn't sure exactly what *it* was. It sounded like a voice . . . a girl's voice whispering in the wind as it brushed by me—calling out from thin air.

Daddy.

I stood perfectly still, listening. Was I going completely bonkers? I wasn't even drunk yet. I waited. Nothing. I chuckled at the absurdity of my hallucination and checked my watch. I had to get going. It was Christmas Eve, and I was behind schedule. I resisted the temptation to toss my mail in the gutter and head straight to the liquor store. There were gifts and last-minute Christmas cards in my bag. I had to make those drops.

I took an awkward step and lost my footing on a patch of ice. My feet splayed out in front of me, my postal bag flew open, and, letters flying, I slammed down on my back—head clunking hard on the frozen cement curb.

Blackness.

CHAPTER SEVENTEEN

When I opened my eyes, there was no more snow, no biting wind or brisk night. I was flat on my back, staring up into a boiling-hot sun. I shielded my eyes, squinting against the glare. I lay there trying to focus, clinging to one of the scattered thoughts that flashed through my head. I was soaked in sweat, my brow moist with perspiration. And someone was with me.

As my eyes adjusted, I could make out a scruffy, darkly bearded man with a deeply tanned face leaning over me. He appeared to be somewhere in his late fifties or early sixties, his face weathered and lined and kind. There was a look of mild concern in his lively eyes. When he saw that I'd opened mine, he smiled, and I could almost feel his relief. Maybe he'd thought I was dead.

"Hello, friend," he said. His voice was rich and wise. "Are you all right?"

I propped myself up on my elbows and got a better look at my Good Samaritan. The man was decked out in a mantle and tunic and wore sandals on his dirt-caked feet. He held a crook in his right hand, and there was a sheepskin sack slung over his shoulder.

Then I looked past him, taking in my surroundings.

Where am I?

When my eyes adjusted to the brightness, all I could see were scrubby rolling hills stretching to a distant horizon. I spotted a flock of sheep grazing nearby, and two curious young men standing a dozen or so yards away, watching me. They were dressed like the man who was standing over me. My thoughts churned as I tried to latch onto something that made sense.

Where did I come from?

A fleeting memory of cold night skipped across my mind. Ice and snow and a stroke of sudden shock. What had happened to me? More than that . . . who *was* me? A strange and disconcerting realization rolled over me like a wave. I had no earthly idea who in the world . . . I was. My heart started to pound, and I felt nauseated and dizzy. Frenzied thoughts bounced off the walls of my mind in a desperate search for something to anchor them. How could I not know my own name, my identity?

The friendly man seemed to notice my disorientation. "My son. Are you all right?"

"Where am I?" I said.

The man extended his hand. "You are here."

I took his hand, and he helped me to my feet. He was strong, his grip firm. I stood unsteadily and silently for a moment, trying to get my bearings, not sure if my legs would support my weight. I looked down. I was dressed like this man and the others, in a dirty white tunic and sandals. I felt my head. A scarf was wrapped around my brow, the tail dangling below my shoulders.

So, is this me? Am I one of . . . them? Whatever they are?

Somehow, the idea felt strange and foreign and . . . wrong. I felt that I was somehow different. But then again, maybe this *was* my life. Maybe I was right where I belonged. But if that were true, then why did a nagging feeling of unfamiliarity haunt me? Why did I feel like a stranger in a foreign land? And why in the world didn't I remember my life?

"I am Isaac," the older man said. When I didn't respond, he gestured toward the others. "These are my sons, Aaron and Teva." The two young men nodded. They seemed to be as mystified by my presence as I was theirs. "We are shepherds."

I nodded. Shepherds. They were shepherds. Was I also a shepherd? "I'm . . ." I didn't quite know what came next. Surely, I had a name. Embarrassed, I felt the blood rush to my cheeks. I must be called something. I strained to remember, as if trying to recall what I'd had for breakfast a week earlier. Nothing came. I looked at the men and shrugged. "I'm sorry. I don't seem to . . . remember my name."

Isaac the shepherd smiled as if he expected as much. "All is well. Perhaps you struck your head when you fell."

"Fell?"

"From your camel," Isaac said. "We surmised that you were thrown and then your camel fled."

I considered the idea. Maybe he was right. Maybe I had fallen. Was that why I couldn't remember anything? But a camel? I certainly couldn't remember a camel.

"I don't know," I said. "Maybe."

I felt the back of my scalp and winced. Sure enough, there was a knot there, tender to the touch. I looked around, perhaps expecting to see my wayward camel grazing nearby. "I guess he's long gone," I said.

Isaac nodded. He looked back at the other shepherds as if he weren't quite sure what to make of me. "So where is your place of birth?"

I stared at him and bit my lip. *Where was I born? Surely, I didn't just drop out of the sky.* "I'm afraid I don't know," I said. "Sorry."

Again, the man looked back at his younger comrades. "Is there anything you know of your life? Anything you can tell us?" Again, I strained and searched my brain, trying to find something useful. I came up empty. My life before that moment was a blank slate. "Look, I know this sounds crazy," I said, "but I've got nothing. No memory beyond waking up a minute ago and finding myself here with you."

The older shepherd moved over to the others, and they huddled for a moment. I couldn't make out what they were saying, but I could tell there was some disagreement among them that was finally settled by the older gentleman. When they broke their huddle, he came back over to me and smiled.

"Well, friend. We are moving our flock back home. Why don't you join us?"

I took a moment to consider my options and realized I had none. "Sure."

◆ ◆ ◆

As sweltering midday turned to torridly hot afternoon, my new shepherd friends and I traversed a rugged path across a rocky hill region that eventually crossed a crest, sloped down a narrow ridge path, and merged into lush grassland crisscrossed by a clear blue meandering river.

I spoke little along the way, mainly because I had no idea what to say. I was lost in my own muddled thoughts as I tried to reassemble the mental puzzle pieces of my murky existence. What had happened to me? How did I get there? The questions made my head pound.

Occasionally, brief glimpses of incoherent images would flash in my mind like a blinking light. Snowfall. Water. A gasp for breath. A sharp pain.

I'd focus for a few minutes but couldn't piece the images together. Was I simply a shepherd who had, in fact, tumbled off his camel? If so, what happened to my flock? Did I have a family? A home? My life was a foggy landscape. *You have to find a way to relax,* I told myself. I was afraid if I didn't quell my anxiety, I was going to pass out, and these kindly shepherds would have to carry me the rest of the way.

In a strange way, it felt as if I'd been born that very day, dropped right out of the sky with no past. A man without a history. But then those flashes would come, impressions that skipped through my head, flickering in and out like fireflies flitting just out of reach—a tuft of red hair, a smile, a little girl's eyes, a flash of pink, a ratty scarf. Were these disjointed images part of who I was?

"So friend," Isaac said. "Tell me about your people."

I looked at him. "My people?"

"Your kinsmen," he said. "Surely, you remember those you love."

"I can't remember much about anything," I said. "I'm sorry."

Isaac nodded sympathetically. "All is well. You will stay with us until you remember."

I looked at him and smiled. I liked this guy. And so I journeyed on with my new friends, an enigmatic traveler whose existence was a riddle with no apparent solution.

CHAPTER EIGHTEEN

It was early evening when we arrived at the shepherd homestead. The cluster of mud-and-straw huts was nestled alongside a bend in the river tucked among a small range of rolling green mountains. As we crested a rise and headed down the final stretch, a bell clanged in the distance. I watched as more than a dozen women and children emerged from the shanties and ran to the center of the encampment to welcome us. I wondered just how long these men had been away from home, as the wholehearted greeting that awaited us suggested they'd been absent for weeks. I'd later learn they'd been out to pasture for only three days, but were celebrated home in such a fashion even if they had been gone on just a night's journey.

Aaron smiled and patted me on the shoulder. "Home," he said.

As we approached, three small boys and two little girls broke from the others and ran to greet us. I knew immediately to whom they belonged by whose arms they leapt into. An older boy took charge of the sheep, herding them into a large pen, while the younger children were full of smiles and chatter and curiosity about the stranger in their midst. I sensed they were examining me, taking my measure, like I was the new kid on the first day of school. I figured strangers were a rare occurrence in such a remote place.

As I watched my new friends reunite with their family, I felt self-conscious and out of place. Isaac sensed this; he walked over and put a fatherly arm around my shoulders. "Welcome," he said. "Our home is now your home."

I smiled and nodded at the inquiring faces around me. Isaac decided I needed a note of explanation. "This is our friend," he said. "We found him lost along the way. A man without a name."

One by one, Isaac's family members approached and introduced themselves. I nodded, said hello, and wondered how I was going to keep their names straight. The last in line was a handsome woman I figured to be in her late forties. She had crystal-clear sky-blue eyes and chestnut hair and seemed so vaguely familiar. Her face was sympathetic and wise and her eyes full of mischief. She cupped my face in her hands and gave me a kiss on the cheek. Then she stepped back and appraised me, as if sizing me up for a new suit.

"He doesn't look lost to me," she said. She took my hands in hers. "Welcome home. I am Joanna, Isaac's wife." She turned to the others. "For now, we will call him Jed—because he is God's friend and a friend to us."

There was something about these good and simple people that made me feel safe. Maybe they could help me remember my life, help me recall who I was and why I was there. The children gathered around me, staring up into my face with curious eyes. I held out my hand, and some of the little ones clasped hold of my dirty fingers. Their touch calmed me, made me feel that maybe, just maybe, all would be well.

"Where's my daughter?" Isaac called out. "Where's Elisabeth? Why has she not come to welcome us home?"

"She has gone to gather figs for supper," Joanna said. She smiled at me. "Perhaps you should bathe before you meet our eldest daughter."

I looked at Isaac hoping for a little more explanation, but he just smiled and nodded. "Go now . . . Jed. Cool off in the river."

I found a quiet spot in a bend in the slow-moving river about a hundred yards from the homestead and dipped my toe. The water was cool. Once I'd made sure I was alone, I peeled off my dirty garments and waded in. It was deeper than it looked, nearly six feet near the middle. The water temperature was perfect, just the right amount of cool to be refreshing. I dunked my head and floated on my back, gazing up at the deep-blue evening sky. A crescent moon was beginning to show her face in the fading light. With my ears submerged, the sound of my breathing was magnified, my heartbeat a whisper in my ears. I took a deep breath and decided that if my memories were to return, I couldn't force them. I had to let them come back in their own good time. Besides, I really had no other choice.

For the time being, I would be Jed, the man who fell from his camel. I felt safe with these good people, and there was one advantage to my memory loss—I had no worries, nothing to trouble my thoughts. I lived in the moment. And something told me the shadowy life I'd left behind hadn't afforded me that luxury.

A pebble plopped near my head and startled me. I righted myself and looked around. Where had it come from? Another small rock plunked in the water, barely missing me. I spotted my assailant. A young woman was sitting on the back of a burro at river's edge. I quickly sunk down in the water to hide my nakedness.

"I'm bathing," I said.

"I can see that," the woman said. The twilight framed her in an ethereal amber glow. She was wearing a clean white tunic and soft leather sandals, but no headdress. Her crimson hair shone like fire in the deep auburn sunset light. Her locks were ornately plaited in a woven crown, her face partially concealed in shadow.

"Do I know you?" I said. It was a legitimate question from a man who didn't even remember his own name. For all I knew, she could be a family member out looking for me. Maybe she'd come to take me home.

"That's a silly question," she said. "How would I know you?"

"I lost my memory," I said. I felt I needed some sort of explanation.

"Oh," she said. "Then I suppose you don't remember why you're swimming in my river?"

I looked around and then down at the water. "I don't see your name on it." *Wow. Did I really just say that?* She stared at me like I'd wandered out of the loony bin. "Sorry," I said. "That was pretty lame."

She gave me a good long look, turned her burro about-face, and rode off toward the homestead.

"Nice to meet you," I called after her. She didn't look back.

◆　◆　◆

By dinner, I knew the identity of my rock-throwing friend from the river. Her name was Elisabeth, and she was Isaac's eldest daughter. She was seated directly across from me at the evening meal and—try as I might to feign disinterest—I couldn't keep my gaze from drifting to her face. In the light of the fire, I was able to get a good look at her features. Her skin was pale with a hint of pink in her lovely cheeks. Her features were soft and girlish. Her lovely smile came easily and often. I watched as she played with the children, laughing at their silliness and showering them with hugs and kisses. They adored her.

There was something so familiar about her: her red hair and pretty face, her soothing voice and easy manner. *I must know her.* But she sure didn't seem to know me. As a matter of fact, she appeared to go out of her way to avoid making eye contact. I didn't take that as an entirely negative sign.

I watched her take Aaron's crying baby from his wife's arms and carry the infant away from the fire.

"This food is delicious," I said.

Joanna smiled at me. "Thank you, Jed." My provisional name, which meant "friend of the Lord," had already caught on. "Elisabeth prepared the lamb," she said. I blushed as if I'd been caught with my hand in the cookie jar. *What is wrong with you, Jed, or whatever your name is? You're acting like a love-struck schoolboy.*

The feast consisted of figs, grapes, olives, fish, bread, and lamb. I was famished and devoured three helpings, much to the delight of the women, who seemed to take my ravenous appetite as a positive review of their culinary expertise. A skin flask filled with wine was passed around the fire. It was warm and sweet and refreshing, yet I could tell it didn't come from grapes. Joanna sensed my confusion.

She smiled as I passed the flask. "Pomegranate."

After the meal, I joined my adopted family around the evening bonfire, where patriarch Isaac called his giddy grandchildren to gather by him for story time.

After the kids had wiggled and wedged their way around their grandfather's feet, Isaac looked up to the night sky and said a prayer of thanks for their many blessings. He finished with "And let us also give thanks to our Heavenly Father for bringing a new friend into our midst. May God's angels help Jed find his way home."

I looked up at the evening sky and wondered where in the world, under that majestic canopy, my home might lie. Was someone looking for me? Did anyone care that I was gone? I looked around the fire at my new friends and felt a surge of warmth. I was lost, but at least I wasn't alone.

◆ ◆ ◆

As Isaac weaved his fanciful tales, I found myself swept up in his rich and engaging storytelling. He told of kings and talking sheep and children who could fly. He told of a man who was several hundred years old who could cure the blind and make the cripples walk. The children's glowing, upturned faces bore evidence that the old shepherd knew what his young audience wanted to hear. However, while the others watched Isaac spin his yarns, I kept an eye on his oldest daughter.

Elisabeth sat near the back of the group with one of the toddler girls nestled in her lap. The little girl was Teva's and looked to be two or three years old. Her eyes were heavy as she struggled to stay awake. Elisabeth had a look of total love and affection on her pretty face as she watched her dad. I figured she'd heard these same stories time and again. Maybe someone had cuddled her when she was little just as she was cuddling her niece. Again, there was an undeniably nagging familiarity in her sparkling hazel eyes and pretty heart-shaped face. It was as if her memory were on the tip of my thoughts, but I could quite conjure it.

This is all too much, I thought. *I need answers. And I need them now!* Immediately, I heard a voice. It was firm and clear and seemed to come out of thin air:

Trust in the Lord with all thine heart; and lean not unto thine own understanding. In all thy ways acknowledge him, and he shall direct thy paths.

I looked around at the others. Surely, they'd heard it, too. But all eyes were still on Isaac as he continued his fireside fables. I rubbed my eyes. *Am I delusional?* But I knew what I'd heard. It was plain as day.

"May I sit by you?"

I looked up to see Elisabeth standing beside me. For a moment, I was as tongue-tied as a clumsy high school freshman on a first date. She'd scarcely glanced my way all evening, and then there she was, standing beside me, waiting for an answer. The words stuck in my throat; I was afraid to open my mouth for fear of what sound might pop out. The shepherd's daughter misinterpreted my hesitation.

"Sorry to disturb." She turned away.

"Yes!" I blurted it out so loudly it caused Isaac to stop abruptly. All heads swiveled in my direction. I felt my cheeks flush. The children giggled. I caught a twinkle in Isaac's eyes. Joanna was smiling at me. I looked up at Elisabeth. She seemed amused by my outburst. Though it was far too late, I still tried to play it cool. "Why not?" I said.

Elisabeth took a seat beside me so close I could feel the fabric of her tunic brush against my arm. Isaac nodded to me and continued. I did my best to pretend I was thoroughly enraptured by his narrative, but I could no longer concentrate on a word he said. I kept stealing glances over at the beautiful young woman beside me. Strangely, it felt as if we'd done this already, as if we'd already lived such a moment, side by side, many times before in some misty other life. I turned to her and whispered.

"All we need are s'mores."

She looked confused. "What are s'mores?"

I stared at her as if I'd completely lost my train of thought. I realized I wasn't sure myself. Where had the word come from? What did it mean? "Nothing . . ." I said. I felt like a fool and silently cursed my vacant memory. But then again, I'd somehow mustered that strange word. Maybe more words would come; maybe if enough of them came tumbling out, I could fit the pieces of my life together.

Elisabeth sensed my discomfort. "It's all right," she whispered. "I sometimes make up words, too."

◆　◆　◆

I spent the night on a bed of straw in a cramped stable in the company of a donkey, a cow, and two goats. Despite my exhaustion, sleep was hard to come by. My mind was clicking on overdrive, working feverishly to fill in the missing details of my hollow life.

Through a gap in the roof, a patch of night sky glimmered, and it brought some measure of comfort. I recalled the words of the mysterious voice I'd heard that evening by the fire . . . *he shall direct thy paths.* Was I on a path? If so, where in the world was it leading me? I prayed for the voice to return, to offer more words of solace and wisdom, but all I could hear were the soft snores of the animals and the sound of the wind gusts slapping the side of the stable.

In the wee hours of the morning, I finally drifted off to sleep only to find that my dreams were as murky and incoherent as my waking thoughts. There were bursts of vague memories: haunting visions of ice and hollow dead eyes and darkness. Then, amid this gloomy vision, a hopeful sign: the cheerful, distinctive sound of a little girl laughing.

CHAPTER NINETEEN

My days and nights spent with my new shepherd friends moved as slowly and lazily as the river that curled through the green valley. Days rolled past, and I lost track of them, as it seemed pointless to count the sunrises and sunsets. What did time matter to a man with no past and no future plans?

I was busy from sunup to nightfall. There was always food to gather or repairs to make or water to tote from the river. I learned how to harvest wheat and barley and chickpeas, how to make porridge, and how to cultivate flax and sesame. I became an expert in threshing and learned how to winnow using a pitchfork and hoe. I was taught how to use the wind to separate the chaff and straw from the grain. My soft hands toughened, and my light skin tanned from the constant work in the heat of day. I eagerly embraced the chores around the homestead. And when it was time to take the sheep to pasture, I willingly tagged along, welcoming the change in routine. It was a contented, happy time, and though my memories didn't return as quickly as I had hoped, I did my best not to stress over it. When I did sink into one of my distant, somber moods, Elisabeth would notice and gently pull me out of it.

"Come back to us, Jed," she'd say. "The memories will come in their own time."

Though I enjoyed the time out at pasture with Isaac, Aaron, and Teva, it was the time at home I cherished most. Sometimes, we'd be gone for a few days, other times a week or even longer. But no matter the duration, there was nothing sweeter than coming over that rise and hearing the clang of the bell signaling our arrival. I would scan the valley below looking for her, trying to pick out those red locks among the excited family members. As we arrived back in our private little village, Elisabeth would first greet her father and brothers and save me for last. She'd approach gently, as if I were still new to her.

"And how was your journey, Jed?"

"Passable," I'd say. "But it's good to be home."

After a time, it did come to feel like home. I was no longer the stranger among them. Each night, I'd join my new family around the fire for supper, songs, and more of Isaac's stories. There were no special days or holidays. Every day was a grateful celebration.

Elisabeth and I grew closer. Each evening, before supper, we'd take a sunset stroll along the path that ran alongside the river. I'd mostly listen as she talked about her hopes and dreams and thoughts on life. She'd inherited her father's storytelling skills, but hers weren't as dramatic or fanciful as her old man's. Elisabeth found humor and meaning everywhere she looked. She had a childlike curiosity about everything that crossed her path. As we walked, she'd stop suddenly to pick up a curiously shaped rock or to point out a certain star in the evening sky. She pondered life and existence and wondered if—somewhere out in the vast blackness of space—there was another woman such as herself, taking a sunset stroll with a man like me.

"Is there a purpose?" she said one evening. "To all of this? Our world? Our lives?"

I shrugged. I wasn't even sure there was a purpose to my own mysterious existence, much less the world at large. "I don't know," I said. She stopped and looked at me.

"I believe there is. There surely must be. There's too much goodness in the world for it all to be some accident."

I wondered what Elisabeth thought of me. While I could tell she enjoyed my company, she still kept me at arm's length, as if something was holding her back, keeping her from letting her guard down. I didn't want to push things. How could I give my heart to someone when I didn't even know whose heart I was giving? Despite the warmth and acceptance I felt among these good people, I couldn't shake the persistent, disconcerting feeling of being a stranger in a strange land. And then there was that inescapable sense that somewhere out there in the vast universe . . . there was someone else. Someone important. Did my heart already belong to another?

◆ ◆ ◆

One night, as I was heading off to bed, Isaac took me aside.

"Jed, we'll be taking the flock to Jerusalem in the morning—to market. We'd like you to come with us."

"Of course," I said. This would my first trip to market, to an actual city. I thought maybe being there could help me learn more about who I was. Maybe I would recognize something or someone that could help me find my way back.

That night, I was visited by another dark vision. In my nightmare I was submerged in freezing water up to my shoulders, a cloudy, frozen ceiling just above my head. The voices of children playing nearby filtered through the thick coat of ice, and I caught blurred visions of movement and flashes of color on the other side. I called out.

"Hey! Anybody hear me? I need help!"

I tapped on the ice lid above my head, but nobody came to my aid. Then the frigid water began to rise: up to my chin, then nose and eyes. My salvation was just a few feet above me, yet no one seemed aware I was there. I breathed in a lungful of water. *I am going to die. So this is what dying feels like.* Then, as the water flowed down my throat to snuff out my life, I awoke, springing up with a desperate gasp, sucking in air in fits and starts.

I took in my surroundings and realized I'd been dreaming. I sat there in the dark and told myself all was well, that I was safe. But then, as my thoughts settled, I wondered. *Was it just a dream?* Or had I experienced a glimpse into my dark and mysterious other life? What if the life I was so desperate to remember was, perhaps, best left forgotten?

◆ ◆ ◆

When I stepped out from my stable room at dawn the next morning, I found the entire village had risen early to see us off.

Elisabeth was sitting astride her burro, dressed for the journey. Isaac, Teva, and Aaron stood by, staffs in hand. The sheep had already been freed from the pen and were meandering along the trail that led down to the river.

"Elisabeth will accompany us," Isaac said.

As though I needed further explanation, Joanna chimed in. "She will buy provisions and medicine for the village." I tried to contain my enthusiasm. Whenever I went out to pasture with the guys, it was Elisabeth I missed the most, and now she was coming with us. I simply nodded, as if it didn't matter to me if she came or not. When I looked up at Elisabeth, she flashed me a sly smile. Despite my feigned nonchalance, she knew I was thrilled she was coming.

"Let us pray," Isaac said. The patriarch bowed his head, and the rest of us followed suit. Isaac's words were familiar, although I wasn't altogether sure where I'd heard them.

"The Lord is my shepherd; I shall not want. He maketh me to lie down in green pastures: he leaded me beside the still waters . . ."

◆　◆　◆

By midday, we'd moved the flock across the river valley, through a canyon, and up a narrow path along a gently sloping range. As we climbed, the air grew cooler, and scattered clouds gave relief from the sweltering sun.

I spent the entire morning walking alongside Elisabeth. I held her donkey's bridle and listened intently as she poured out her heart to a man she barely knew. I found her voice comforting, and her dreams refreshing. They were humble, simple aspirations with no illusions of glory or grandeur. She hoped to marry a good man and make a home beside her parents and brothers and their families. She was perfectly content to live there by that river for the rest of her life.

"How old are you?" I said, immediately wondering if I'd overstepped.

"Twenty." She didn't seem to mind the question.

"Oh, you have plenty of time for all that," I said. She took my measure.

"Jed, are you mocking me?"

"Mocking you? No. I meant . . . you're young, that's all. You've got your whole life ahead of you. Marriage is a big step. Right?"

"My mother married at fourteen," Elisabeth said. "Teva's wife, Sarah, was thirteen."

"Really?" I said. "Married at thirteen?"

Elisabeth frowned. "And what is wrong with that?"

"Nothing," I said. I'd backed myself into a corner. "I . . . let's just say where I come from, that's a bit young."

"I thought you didn't know where you came from," she said. She had me there. How was it that I had a view on the correct marrying age?

I seemed to know lots of things, had opinions and thoughts—I just had no idea where or how they'd formed. There was a black hole where my life experience should be.

Elisabeth let my faux pas slide and moved on. "Perhaps, in time, you will remember more about your life," she said. "Do you think it's possible that you have a wife and family?"

I shrugged. "Wish I could tell you."

"What do you think she's like?" she asked. "If you have a wife, that is."

I laughed. "You want me to imagine a wife that I may or may not have?"

"Yes," she said. "I'd like to hear what wife you would imagine."

"Well," I said, "I suppose she'd be very large and strong. Maybe the size of Aaron or larger. With big shoulders."

She gave me a look that said she knew I was pulling her leg. "And why do you want a wife that looks like my brother?"

"Well, so that she can do all the work while I take long baths in the river and sleep under the shade tree."

"Ah," she said. "You seek a life of leisure."

"Doesn't everybody?" I said. "I mean . . . there's a lot to be said for leisure."

Elisabeth thought about this for a moment. "I couldn't be happy unless I was doing something. I think I'm happiest when I'm cooking or washing clothes at the river. That's why I sing while I work, because I feel—when I'm doing those things—I have purpose. My life has value."

I pondered her words until I had a flash of insight. "Something tells me that in my other life, my work involved . . . carrying something."

Elisabeth nodded. "Well, maybe you carried water for your village."

I smiled. I really didn't think that was it. "Maybe." I looked at her. "You better hope I remember my life. If not, you may be stuck with me forever."

Elisabeth smiled and looked straight ahead. "I can think of worse fates."

◆ ◆ ◆

"We'll pitch camp here," Isaac said.

We'd been on the trail all day, and I was dirty and tired and famished. The sun had just slipped below the distant mountain range. Our campsite near the rim of a plateau looked out over a sprawling savannah that stretched to a deep purple sunset horizon.

While the others pitched camp and Elisabeth set about preparing our evening meal, I sat on a rock at the edge of the ridge and took in the panoramic view. We were surrounded by fertile pastureland, the perfect spot to park the flock for a night's rest. I kept watch as the last light of day drained from the skyline. In the distance, I could barely make out the faint flickering of lights.

"Jerusalem."

I turned to see Aaron standing beside me. He put a hand on my shoulder. "Come, Jed. Elisabeth has prepared us victuals for supper."

Elisabeth's meal consisted of bread and pomegranates. The fruit was the perfect mixture of tart and sweet and tasted a bit like cranberries. We passed around a flask of bittersweet pomegranate wine. It had been a long and exhausting day for everyone, so words were few as we sat around the fire sharing in the food Elisabeth had prepared. I caught her eye and nodded, letting her know I thought she'd done a good job. She flashed a grateful smile.

"Jed told me a story today," Elisabeth said. The three men all looked at me.

"Oh?" Teva said. "Was it a good story?"

"I think so," Elisabeth said. "I think it might be the best story I've ever heard." The shepherds laughed.

"My sister speaks with high praise," Aaron said.

"Father, it looks like your oratory has a rival," Teva said.

"Well then, I fear I am envious," Isaac said. "I have told my daughter many stories, and yet our friend Jed has trumped me at first telling." The older shepherd smiled. "Please. Let us also hear your tale, Jed."

"Yes, let's hear it," Aaron said.

"It's not even my story," I said. "At least I don't think it is." The truth was I wasn't even sure how I knew the story or where I'd heard it—only that it was in my head. Whether it was a tale of my own creation or borrowed from a wiser teller, I wasn't sure.

I'd told Elisabeth my anecdote simply to pass the time, happy that I had something stored in my memory I could share. She'd scarcely responded when I'd finished, so I thought she hadn't cared for it.

I glanced at Elisabeth to find her smiling at me.

"Stop delaying," she said. "Tell them as you told me."

I could tell by their expressions there was no getting out of it. I rubbed my hands over the fire, stalling for time as I gathered my thoughts.

"Okay," I began. "Here goes. This is the story of a Good Samaritan. Once upon a time there was a man walking the road from Jerusalem to Jericho. And as he went, he was accosted by thieves . . ."

I told the tale of brotherly love as it came to me. It felt so familiar, yet I was pretty sure I had not concocted it on my own. Could this be a story I'd once heard, or had I, like Isaac, been the storyteller in my family? Had I simply made this tale up to entertain my own children? As I spoke, my shepherd friends leaned forward, listening intently. Elisabeth too was watching me with an interest I hadn't sensed the first time I'd told it on the trail that day.

After I finished, I looked up at my audience of four. Their faces were still and thoughtful, and I couldn't quite tell if they liked the story or not. Then Isaac slowly nodded.

"Your story—it is a lesson for life," he said. "It is our duty to look after even the least among God's children."

I nodded. He'd nailed it. We sat in silence for a moment, and then Isaac launched into a tale of his own: a fable about a small boy who cleverly outfoxes a Roman centurion. I was grateful to be out of the spotlight. When I caught Elisabeth studying me, she smiled and looked away. I felt a surge of joy. I had no idea who I was or where I came from, but one thing I knew for certain . . . I was thoroughly entranced.

CHAPTER TWENTY

That night I volunteered for the late shift watching over the flock. It was an easy gig. The sheep slept peacefully and undisturbed in a pasture a stone's throw from the campsite.

It was a pitch-black, moonless night, and sitting on a rock gazing up at the shimmering night sky, I felt at peace. A light breeze blew up from the valley below and brought cool comfort. I relished the stillness and tranquility of the moment, but my calm was short-lived as—again—flashes of my former life pirouetted through my mind. I saw the face of a young girl, her long red hair flowing over narrow shoulders. She was smiling, laughing, her face aglow, her eyes dancing and joyful. Then her face suddenly changed. The light drained from her eyes. They flew open in terror as she reached, grasped for me. I held out my hand, tried to take hers, but she was just out of range. And then she was gone, the vision zapped into the blackness.

"Who are you?" I said aloud. "And why do you haunt me so?"

"To whom are you speaking?"

I turned toward the voice to see Elisabeth's outline, a shawl draped over her shoulders. She motioned for me to move over and hoisted herself up beside me on the boulder.

"Nobody," I said. "I talk to myself sometimes."

"Oh," Elisabeth said. "I do this, as well. Only, when I speak to no one in particular, I'm not really conversing with myself; I'm talking to God."

"Does he answer you?"

"Yes," she said. "He always answers me. But it's not always the answer I wish to hear."

I smiled and nodded. "I know what you mean."

"So, you remember God, at least?" she said.

I nodded. "Yes. But I don't remember how I know him—or even if I believe in him."

"Believe in him?" she said. It was as if the concept was too peculiar for her to comprehend. "How can one not believe in him?"

I smiled. "I have a feeling . . . though I can't know for sure . . . that where I come from, there are lots of people who don't believe. Or at least aren't sure if he exists."

Elisabeth regarded me with the most bemused look on her sweet face. "Do you believe in the sunrise?" she asked.

"The sunrise? Well, of course I believe in the sunrise."

"Why do you believe in the sunrise?"

"Because I see it every morning. And even when I don't see it, I know it happened because I wake up and see the sun in the sky."

"How can you be so sure of the sunrise, but doubt the God that creates the sun and commands it to rise and set, the God that brings the rain and makes the rivers flow? This idea seems awfully silly to me, Jed."

I laughed. When she put it that way, it did seem a bit silly. "You have a good point," I said. "I'm sorry. Losing my memory has made me a little confused about things. Well, maybe a *lot* confused."

"I've heard tell of those who lost their memory because there was something they didn't want to remember," Elisabeth said. "Do you think this might be true in your case, Jed?"

I sighed, considering the idea. "I guess it's possible. I want to know my life, but a part of me is afraid to. What if you're right? What if there is something in my past too terrible to remember?"

Elisabeth looked up at the night sky. I studied her, drinking her in: the curve of her smooth neck, the way her hair fell about her shoulders, the sweet half smile on her perfect lips. I wanted to burn her face into my memory. A gentle breeze blew through her hair, and she closed her eyes and relished it. I thought about how she appreciated every little thing life had to offer. There was something about her that brought me hope. She made me feel as if everything was going to be all right. Finally, she turned and looked at me.

"Jed, you are not like any man I've ever known."

"I hope that's a compliment," I said.

"Merely an observation," Elisabeth said. "You seem to me like a man from another time. The future, perhaps."

I nodded. The truth was, I'd also felt that. Lying in my stable room at night, I'd imagined I had come from some future time and world to this place. For what reason, I had no idea. But even though my memory hadn't made the journey with me, I was glad I had come. For Elisabeth was there waiting for me, and I wanted to stay with her forever.

"The future," I said. "Far into the future. I sometimes think maybe I've come from a time yet to be conceived." I didn't know where that idea had come from. The thought popped into my head and then made its way south to my tongue. But how could I know such a thing? It seemed such foolish conjecture.

"Tell me . . ." Elisabeth said. "Do people still fall in love in this future world? Do they dance to celebrate a bountiful harvest? Do they sing songs and share stories around the fire?"

I thought it over. "Yes. I think so. I feel sure that love and joy still exist. At least, I hope they do. If my memory ever comes back, I'll tell you for sure."

Elisabeth smiled. "If you could take me to this future world . . . would you? Just for a visit?"

I looked into her eyes. That was the easiest question anyone had ever asked me. "Yes, Rebecca. I'd take you in a minute."

Elisabeth turned to me with a curious look on her face. "What did you call me?"

I had no idea what she was talking about. "I called you . . . Elisabeth. Your name."

"No. You said *Rebecca*. Who's Rebecca?"

I felt a knot in my stomach. Where had the name come from? Who was Rebecca? I hadn't a clue. "I don't know," I said. "I don't know any Rebecca. At least . . . I don't think I do."

Elisabeth gave me long searching look. "Perhaps she is someone from your mysterious future world. Maybe she's trying to climb out of your memory."

I bit my lower lip. *Rebecca*. The name had rolled off my tongue effortlessly, as if I'd said it a hundred times before. Was she a friend? A relative? I felt a surge of frustration. "I'm afraid I don't know."

Elisabeth touched my arm. "It's all right. I think it's a good omen. Perhaps your memory is returning. Perhaps more names will come, maybe even your own."

Suddenly, a strange tingling scurried up my spine. The hairs on the back of my neck and arms stood up, drawn by some mysterious magnetic force. I felt light, almost weightless. My tear ducts beaded up like water droplets on a flower petal.

Something is . . . happening.

All at once, the murky night came into focus. I could see everything so clearly. I looked over at Elisabeth, and the puzzled look on her face said she was experiencing the same mystical something. I held out my arm and showed her the tiny hairs all standing at attention.

"What's happening?" Elisabeth asked. In the meadow, the sheep stirred and began to bleat, their heads arcing skyward.

166

All around us appeared a strange dark purple glow. I stretched my hand out, and my fingers were luminescent. So were the rocks and fields and sheep. Elisabeth was glowing, her red hair a light unto itself. Her lovely hazel eyes blazed with this strange and mysterious spark. She looked at me with the face of a little girl, her countenance radiant with joyous wonder at some new and magnificent discovery.

"Jed, look at you!" she said. "You're glowing!" She looked down at her fingertips. "And so am I! Everything's glowing!"

I smiled. If ever there was a feeling of pure, undiluted bliss, I was feeling it. I tried to make sense of what was happening, but this was an experience no mere words could convey. It was simply too mind-bogglingly extraordinary. But it was happening. It was real.

In the fields around us, the sheep felt it, too. They were frisky and full of vigor like newborn lambs.

"Look!" Elisabeth said. I followed her upward gaze. There, hovering above us, was the aurora borealis, an exquisite kaleidoscope of lavender, scarlet, and emerald.

"Yes," I whispered. "The northern lights."

As Elisabeth and I stared up in astonishment, we saw a tiny point of bright white light form at the center of the phenomenon. It was faint at first, barely discernible among the magnificent display of color.

Then—as if some invisible finger flipped a switch—the tiny light began to expand, growing larger and larger, brighter and brighter until it washed away the wavy lights of the aurora and exploded in a white-hot supernova. With Elisabeth by my side, I sat dumbstruck and watched a new star born: a star that swelled and expanded until it was large and vivid, like a thousand constellations all rolled into one. It loomed large and glorious in the eastern sky, four brilliant points jutting out thin spires of radiance to form a cross.

Elisabeth gasped in awe.

The magnificent megastar shone its glorious beams on the fields all around us and brought a feeling of warmth and comfort, an intense sensation of inexplicable tranquility. The happiest moments of my life had been gathered like seeds and scattered into my mind all at once. The light was *alive*. And rather than millions of miles away, it seemed to be lingering just above us in the night sky, within range of a good bowshot.

The sheep grew quiet, likely dumbstruck by the wonder of it all, their necks craned upward, gawking at the new star illuminating the night.

"Oh, Jed," Elisabeth said. "The star . . . I think I've died and gone to heaven. Only I never imagined heaven so wonderful as this."

"Yes," I said. "I've never felt this way before. It's as though . . ."

"Nothing else matters." Elisabeth finished my thought as naturally as if my thinking were merely an extension of her own. "What's happening?" she asked.

"I don't know." Then I realized that she hadn't spoken the words at all. She'd thought them, and I'd heard them and responded in my own thoughts.

I turned and saw that Isaac, Teva, and Aaron had joined us.

"The star of Bethlehem," I heard someone whisper and realized the voice was my own.

"It's a miracle," Isaac said. "A sign from God."

"Yeah," I said. "A sign of good things to come." I felt warmth on my skin, and realized that Elisabeth had slipped her hand into mine. Tears rolled freely down my face. Tears of wonder. Tears of joy.

Field and fountain, moor and mountain, following yonder star.

So, this is it, I thought. *This is what peace on earth feels like.* I was again aware of a strange lightness of being. The tension in my stomach and chest and mind—a sensation I'd carried so long I'd stopped noticing its weight—was no longer there. The underlying fear that had always hovered within me and gripped my inner being was simply gone.

And then the giant star flared out in a burst of intense brightness that seemed to be aimed right at us. I shielded my eyes as we were engulfed in a shaft of brilliant starlight.

"The light blinds me," I heard Aaron say. I couldn't see him, couldn't see anyone. There was only that all-absorbing light.

"Father, what does this mean?" Teva said. I could hear the awe in his voice.

"I do not know," Isaac said. "But I feel it must be a wondrous thing to make my heart so leap within me."

"Yes," Elisabeth said. "Wondrous."

When they saw the star they rejoiced with exceeding great joy.

At that moment, a penetrating awareness shot through me, like someone had downloaded every thought and memory I'd ever had back into my mind, the images flickering by like an album of my life. The *me* that I'd forgotten rushed back in like water through a ruptured dam.

I was Paul Thomas Bennett of Manchester, Maine. I was a mail carrier, and I lived in the early part of the twenty-first century. I was married to Rebecca Anne Waverly from the Upper East Side of Manhattan. We'd had two little girls—Megan and Abbey—and a house on Bethlehem Place. Our home. I'd had a family, a wonderful life, and I'd lost everything. Our Megan had died, and I'd felt the pain so deeply I'd lost my way. I'd lost my hope and faith. My pain and anger had destroyed what was left of our family. It was my fault.

Then came flashes of my final hours. An approaching snowstorm. A strange woman in the square. My head hitting the curb.

I had died. I was dead. I had to be. But where was I? Was this heaven? If it was heaven, it certainly wasn't what I'd imagined. Who were these people? Were they dead, too? And if they were, did they know they were dead? The questions popped into my head in rapid succession, but there was no sense of stress or urgency attached to them. And though I had suddenly remembered all the dark details of my gloomy life, I still felt that sense of peace. The cascading thoughts didn't dim my joyous mood in the least. Standing in that glorious starlight protected me from pain and despair; I was sealed off from anything that might do me harm. The grief, recrimination, and guilt couldn't exist in that light. The voice returned to whisper in my mind:

You are my beloved child. And I will care for you.

I suddenly knew where I was and why. I was living out the story from the New Testament, the one Pastor Joe read every Christmas Eve. The greatest story ever told.

Now in the sixth month the angel Gabriel was sent by God to a city of Galilee named Nazareth, to a virgin betrothed to a man whose name was Joseph, of the house of David. The virgin's name was Mary.

Standing there in that surreal moment, I realized I'd never really believed the story to be true. Even in happy times, I'd had my doubts—though I'd never voiced them. But the story was true, and by some strange twist of fate, I was living it. I was there with these simple shepherds as it happened some two thousand years before I was born. The Christmas star—the most beautiful star the sky had ever shone—was real. I softly sang an old familiar tune.

"O star of wonder, star of night. Star with royal beauty bright . . . westward leading, still proceeding, guide us to thy perfect light."

"Jed, that's beautiful," Elisabeth said.

Her face flushed with starlight.

"*Paul*," I said. "My name is Paul Thomas Bennett, and I'm from Manchester, Maine. United States of America."

She smiled. "Paul."

Her familiarity was no longer a mystery. The feelings I thought I had for this pretty young woman weren't for her at all. They belonged to someone else, someone I'd lost: the only woman I'd ever loved and ever would love.

"Rebecca," I whispered to her. Elisabeth smiled at me as if she didn't hear, her dazzling eyes sparkling in the glow. Or maybe she had heard and . . . she *knew*.

Then, out of the tunnel of light came a voice. It was warm and comforting and familiar. It was the same bold voice I'd been hearing in my head ever since the stormy summer day I plunged into a lake to help save a scared little girl.

Fear not. For behold I bring you good tidings of great joy, which shall be to all people. For unto you is born this day in the city of David a savior, which is Christ the Lord. And this shall be a sign unto you; ye shall find the babe wrapped in swaddling clothes, lying in a manger.

I felt another rush of joy so intense I thought I might spread my arms and fly right up into the heavens. Elisabeth and the shepherds laughed—they were feeling it, too. I felt reborn at that very moment, as though every experience, every moment of my mortal life had been a lie—the pathetic counterfeit of a reality too wonderful to comprehend. In that instant, I was gifted a glimpse of life as it truly was, as it truly *felt*, and it was infinitely greater and more perfect than anything I could ever imagine. I wanted so desperately to stay in that moment, to feel that way forever, but I knew in my heart the feeling was fleeting. So I determined to cherish every second.

Above us, a chorus of angelic singers, hundreds, thousands, began a heavenly serenade that reverberated across the night sky. I sang those hymns of soulful celebration along with them and—much to my surprise—I knew the words.

As the choir swelled, the voice returned, thundering with power and force.

Glory to God in the highest, and on earth peace, good will toward men.

As suddenly as they appeared, the angel singers vanished with a wisp into the night air. We were left with vacant stillness.

We all stood still, our sandaled feet unmoving on the desert floor, overwhelmed by what we'd witnessed. *If I ever go back home,* I thought, *I can never breathe a word of this night. If I do, they'll lock me up in the nut house and throw away the key.*

Teva broke the silence. "The City of David."

"Yes," Isaac said. "Bethlehem. We must go see this thing that the angel has told us of. We will leave at first light."

"But what about our flock?" Aaron said. "What about the market?"

"They have shearers in Bethlehem as well as Jerusalem," Elisabeth said. "Perhaps they will even pay more." They all turned to me as if I were the one with the final say, as if I needed to bless the mission with my pearls of wisdom.

"Let's do it," I said.

And that night I dreamed a beautiful dream.

CHAPTER TWENTY-ONE

When the winter sun sets on Wollman Rink in Central Park, the lights from the towering buildings along Fifth Avenue cast an amber glow and make it seem as if the ice is on fire. It was New Year's Eve, and Rebecca looked like a ginger angel as she cut lazy circles in and around the crush of skaters. I watched her effortless glide: her eyes closed, her head back, lost in her own world. I couldn't believe how beautiful she looked. I patted my coat pocket to make sure the ring was still there, as I'd done at least two dozen times that day. I'd been sitting on my big romantic plan for weeks, rehearsing my lines time and again in my head, looking for flaws, trying to predict potential pitfalls. The moment had to be perfect.

The announcer crackled over the loudspeaker: "The rink will close in five minutes."

The skaters started moving to the rail as the rink quickly thinned out. I knew Rebecca would hold out to the bitter end; she loved having the ice to herself even if only for a few waning moments. Nervous knots clenched my stomach. I had never been more scared in my life. It was going to fail. My big plan was going to fall flat on its big, fat face.

"Do it, you big chicken," I said aloud. "Do it now."

I looked around. We were the only skaters left. Soon, the announcer would come back over the speaker, tell us to clear off. *This is it,* I thought. *The moment of truth.* As if she'd read my thoughts, Rebecca turned and skated over to me, skidding to a perfect stop, a cheerful grin dimpling her frost-kissed cheeks.

"I never want to leave here," she said. "Never." She kissed me on the lips. "C'mon! Skate with me one last time this year." She tried to pull me with her, but I dug in my blades.

"Rebecca. No."

She gave me a puzzled look. "Paul? What's wrong?"

I took a deep breath and dipped down on one knee. I knew this was it; there was no turning back. My whole life was now laid out before me. I was as vulnerable as a newborn chick and was about to put my novice heart entirely in her gloved hands.

And then the fear left. A sensation of calm wafted over me like a warm breeze. I felt at peace, as if what I was about to do was divinely ordained, and I had no choice in the matter. *This is right,* I thought. *I know it's right.* It became clear to me that I hadn't created or planned that moment at all. It had been planned for me, and I was just an actor in God's play. And all I needed to do was act . . . and trust.

I took one of Becca's mittened hands in mine and watched the look on her face change. The euphoric glow gave way to bewilderment. I had done it. I had taken my Becca by surprise.

I awkwardly fished around in my coat pocket, retrieved the little felt ring box, and promptly fumbled it to the ice.

"Shoot! Sorry."

I should have been flustered, should have felt foolish, but instead, I was cool and collected and eerily calm. I could almost hear a voice whisper in my ear. *I've got your back, Bennett. Don't worry. You can't mess this up.* I chuckled and picked up the box. Rebecca stared down at me, eyes wide, mouth pinched in a question. I noticed the other skaters and bystanders had picked up the gist of what was transpiring and were forming up on the outside of the rink wall. It was New Year's Eve, and we were giving them a show.

I locked eyes with a middle-aged black man. He winked at me and nodded as if to say, "Buck up boy. You can do it." I suddenly flashed back to my father and mother dancing in the rain on prom night. I felt linked to that moment, to them. And then I felt my mother's presence, beside me on the ice with a hand on my shoulder.

Rebecca's cheeks flushed a rosy pink. I wasn't tongue-tied; I simply wanted to let the moment linger. But I had a pretty girl standing over me, and an eager audience waiting for me to get on with it.

The ice cut into my knee. My left foot was falling asleep. I cleared my throat and popped open the ring box to reveal the pathetic $19.99 cubic zirconia ring I'd picked up at Kmart. I hoped Rebecca wouldn't laugh at my pitiful effort, for it would have to suffice until I could afford something better. I carefully pinched the cheap ring between my thumb and forefinger and clasped her left hand. I peeled off her mitten and coolly tossed it aside.

"Sorry about the ring," I said. "It's only temp—"

"Shhh," Rebecca whispered. "Don't spoil the moment."

As I attempted to slip the ring onto her trembling finger, my cool-headedness was again tested. It was two sizes too small.

"Think we're going to need some butter," I said. I looked around at the audience as if one of them might be holding a stick of Land O'Lakes.

"It's okay," Rebecca said. She took the little ring from me, slipped off her necklace, looped the ring on the end, and draped the pendant back over her neck. She was even cooler than I was. I could feel the eyes on my back, but I didn't care. I only cared about one thing—Becca's answer to the question I was about to pose.

"Rebecca, I love you. I love you more than life. Will you marry me?"

Rebecca's eyes welled up, and her lower lip started to quiver. I'd never seen her cry before. Not once. Not even when her hamster,

Harvey, died. The pooling tears finally broke loose and streamed down her lovely flushed face. Then, she nodded like a bobblehead and spread her arms wide.

I suddenly felt as if I could conquer any challenge, overcome any obstacle, as if I could spread my wings and fly right up to heaven. I swept her up in my arms and twirled her round and round on the ice as the skaters of Wollman Rink cheered. It was the single happiest moment of my life.

And then a chorus rose up from among our fans, a wellspring of harmonic spontaneity. They began to sing, strangers united in song to celebrate two young and foolishly romantic kids starting out on a new and terrifying journey. Their voices swelled to a rousing New Year's blessing, lifting our spirits as we prepared to step into our uncertain future. And it was a most fitting song at that:

> Should old acquaintance be forgot?
> and never brought to mind?
> Should old acquaintance be forgot,
> and auld lang syne?

◆　◆　◆

A gentle tugging on my leg woke me at dawn. "Wake up," Elisabeth said. "We're leaving for Bethlehem." She pointed at the star lingering in the morning sky. "The star has stayed."

"So it wasn't a dream," I said.

Elisabeth smiled. "Come, Paul. We must make haste."

Paul. I was Paul. I had a name again, and a life and a past. The star had stirred my memory awake, and there I was—lost in time, traveling with the famed shepherds of biblical lore.

And there were in the same country shepherds abiding in the field, keeping watch over their flock by night.

I got to my feet and stretched my arms above my head, ready to continue my journey in a world of impossibility—a world that felt more real than the life I'd left behind in Manchester.

As dawn peeked over the horizon, the Bethlehem star remained, and even in the full light of day, it still shone, lingering above as a brilliant companion to the sun in the eastern sky, guiding our way.

The journey to Bethlehem took us along a narrow rocky path. I wondered if this was the same route that Joseph and Mary traveled. I could almost see the young Virgin Mother, in the final hours of her pregnancy, sitting atop the donkey as Joseph led the way. I pictured her so young and afraid. So far from home. I imagined Joseph offering words of comfort, quelling her thirst with his flask, assuring his pregnant wife that all would be well.

The sheep moved ahead of us, their gait quick and energetic. Perhaps they too couldn't wait to get to Bethlehem. Occasionally, they'd turn their heads back as if to say, "What's keeping you?"

I was manning my usual post, holding the reins of Elisabeth's trusty burro. Isaac, Aaron, and Teva were spread out among the flock.

"How far is it to Bethlehem?" I asked Elisabeth.

"Two days' journey," she said.

"I mean in miles."

Elisabeth smiled and shook her head. "You speak in terms I don't comprehend."

"Okay," I said. "Two days' journey. By the way, I now remember how to make s'mores."

"Well, then you must make me one," she said.

I smiled. "Wish I could. Don't think I'm gonna find any marshmallows out here—much less chocolate and graham crackers. Unless we run into a 7-Eleven."

Elisabeth gave me the whimsical look I'd come to learn was her "now you're talking crazy" face. I surmised that if I had to leave this place and time—as I sensed I soon would—I was going to miss that face most of all.

As we moved along, I felt tempted to pour out my life and secrets to Elisabeth. But as I formed the sentences in my head and tried to find ways to make her understand, I realized how futile it all was. How do you explain a smartphone to someone who couldn't comprehend a simple typewriter? How do you describe how a car works or how we put a man on the moon? So I sputtered out generalizations about the world from whence I'd come, doing my best to avoid delving into the nuances of space travel, combustion engines, and the Internet. Finally, I took a breath, and she looked down at me.

"And what of your family? Why have you not yet spoken of them?" I took a moment to gather my thoughts. I wasn't sure how much I should tell her. "Is the subject painful for you?" Elisabeth asked, watching me closely.

"I did have a family," I said. "My wife was named Rebecca, and we had two daughters, Megan and Abigail." An odd feeling came over me as I spoke. I felt nostalgia and regret, but the intense grief that had so gripped my soul back in Manchester was no longer there. I couldn't understand it. How could I be so unfeeling about something so tragic, so horribly devastating? I glanced up at the star and instinctively knew that it had something to do with my transformation. There was something in that light that eased my pain.

"And where are they now?" Elisabeth said.

"They . . ." I wasn't sure how to answer her question. "Megan . . . died."

"Oh," Elisabeth said. "I'm sorry." She took a moment to consider this. "And what of Rebecca and Abigail?"

"They're . . ." I knew there was no point trying to explain. "I'm not exactly sure where they are."

"I imagine you miss them," Elisabeth said. I was relieved she didn't press for more details.

"Yes," I said. I wanted a change of subject. Aaron took care of it for me.

"Bethlehem!" he called out.

I squinted into the late afternoon sun, and sure enough, there it was in the distance, the low structures barely distinguishable from the desert that surrounded it.

As we pushed to cover as much ground as we could before darkness set in, I noticed something unusual. We'd been at a good clip for more than nine hours, and not only did I not feel weary, I felt as rested and refreshed as when we had started our journey that morning. My water flask was still full. I hadn't taken a single swig. I looked up at the star that moved before us. Something told me that it was, again, the culprit. Elisabeth looked at me as if she could read my thoughts.

"The star is alive," she said. "It seems to be watching over us, helping us along. Tell me, Paul. Has God come back to you?"

I looked up at her and smiled. "Yes. I'd say he's made his presence known."

CHAPTER
TWENTY-TWO

"We'll sleep here tonight."

It was just after sunset when Isaac raised his crook to signal the day's journey had come to an end. Bethlehem loomed so close—I could nearly see the flicker of flames from the torches. The wind was blowing our direction, bringing a bitter mixture of scents from the desert city.

As we pitched camp, my eyes drifted up to our friendly neighborhood star. I never tired of looking at it. Like Elisabeth's sweet countenance, I wanted to burn it into my memory, because I sensed that it too would soon be gone from my life. I determined to breathe in and consume every moment of my strange and wonderful passage to Bethlehem. Someday, if I ever got back home, I'd take Pastor Joe to lunch and tell him all about it.

After dinner, I sat on the edge of a ridge with Elisabeth and gazed at the glowing lantern lights of Bethlehem in the distance. The star seemed to be resting just above the desert town. I was moved to speak the words of a favorite old carol . . .

"O little town of Bethlehem, how still we see thee lie! Above your deep and dreamless sleep, the silent stars go by."

Elisabeth smiled. "I like that. Did you write it?"

I chuckled and shook my head. "No. It's a popular song back home—in Manchester—at Christmastime."

"What is Christmastime?"

Her innocent expression told me she was serious. Of course, she wouldn't know about Christmas. "*This* is Christmastime," I said. "The very first Christmas. Christmas celebrates the birth of our savior." I nodded toward Bethlehem. "The baby we're on our way to see."

"And you celebrate Christmas where you come from?"

"We do."

"Even far into the future?" she said.

"Yes," I said. "It's the most important day of the year. At least it's supposed to be. I guess some think it's been corrupted a bit, though."

"What do you mean?" Elisabeth said.

"It's not as much about *this* moment anymore," I said. "People have forgotten that Christmas is about this . . . this journey to see a baby born, a baby that will . . ." I stopped. *I must sound crazy to her. This must be too much for her to process.*

"Save the world," she finished for me. In her heart, she *knew*. She knew what it was we were journeying to witness and sensed the importance of the moment. "Tell me about your village," she said. "How do they commemorate this Christmas there?"

"Well," I said. "Manchester's a small town, and small towns really know how to do Christmas right. Most everybody decorates their home with things that . . . honor Christmas. There are special trees and wreaths and special foods and lights—"

"Lights?" Elisabeth said. I realized I'd ventured into the intricacies of electricity.

"Where I come from—*when* I come from—they've figured out a way to actually *make* light." Elisabeth looked confused. "It's complicated," I said.

"Tell me more about your town."

"Well, it's nice there. People look out for one another. There's a sense of family and fellowship."

"I think I might like this Manchester," Elisabeth said. "Perhaps I will visit someday—at Christmastime."

I smiled. "You sure? It's very cold that time of year."

"I will bring an extra cloak," she said.

"All right," I said. "It's a date."

Elisabeth was silent for a time. When she spoke again, the playfulness was gone. She seemed a little sad. "Do you miss it?" she asked. "Home?"

I took a moment to consider her question. "Not right now," I said. "I'm right where I want to be."

Elisabeth searched my face as if trying to figure out a puzzle. "I should turn in," she said as she rose to her feet. "Good night, Paul."

"Night," I said. As I listened to her footfalls move away, I looked up at the shimmering star. Oddly, I could hear Madonna in my mind, singing a song from *Evita*, the past and the present blurring together in one perfect moment.

Deep in my heart I'm concealing things that I'm longing to say.

Scared to confess what I'm feeling—frightened you'll slip away.

As the tune died in my head, I wondered why I'd thought of that song, one that I'd never considered a favorite, although Rebecca liked it. Maybe I was afraid of losing this peace, that bright star shining down on me with a light I never knew existed. I dug a toe in the desert sand and thought of my bag of mail back home, the liquor store, and the stillness of the air around Megan's grave. I looked up at the star again, realizing my fear was something else entirely, and it was more than this moment I feared losing.

Later that night, while the others slept nearby, I lingered by the campfire, keeping one eye on the flock. I poked the glowing embers with a stick and pondered my fate. *What lies ahead tomorrow when we arrive in Bethlehem? And what will become of me after?* As if eavesdropping on my thoughts, the mysterious voice answered from the fading flames:

Be still, and know that I am God.

Be still.

I closed my eyes and thought about how difficult it had been to find stillness in my life. Each morning since that awful Christmas Day, I'd awakened with a knot of fear in my stomach. Fear of dying. Fear of living. Fear of my own haunting thoughts. Part of me had never left the edge of Waller's Pond.

Then I'd awakened in this strange desert land, not sure if I was dead or alive, not knowing who or where I was or why I was there. And I'd found peace. The stress knots had dissolved, and the constant fear had faded into memory. I felt comforted. And even after my memories had returned, the sense of tranquility stayed. I looked up at the star and whispered.

"Come to me, all who are weary and heavy-laden, and I will give you rest. Be still and know that I am God."

And then—the stillness was shattered.

The earth began to rumble and shake, the logs and rocks around the campfire vibrated, and the sheep scattered, startled by the unseen force descending on us.

The thunder of horse hooves pierced the dark. Isaac and sons leapt to their feet. Elisabeth sat up and peered into the darkness, her eyes fearful. I held out my hand and pulled her up as a dozen Roman cavalrymen rode up and encircled us. The dust and clamor of their swift approach gave way to an uneasy silence. My heart thumped in my chest. There was something ominous and disconcerting about the way the armored soldiers locked on us with steely glares, taking our measure. I looked them over and, strangely, recognized their uniforms from a report on the Roman army I'd done in ninth grade. The men—though tall in the saddle—were shorter than I'd imagined. However, with their gold-plated helmets and swords, they looked pretty close to the drawings I'd once torn from an encyclopedia and taped to a foam-core display board for a history project.

Sitting tall astride a solid white mount, a handsome dark-haired soldier with piercing black eyes glared at me. Did he sense I didn't belong there? He observed me, reading my body language, so I kept my gaze on him to show I had nothing to hide. I knew enough from that long-ago mediocre history report I'd written that the transverse crest on his helmet meant he was a centurion and the leader of the detachment. He gripped the handle of the glinting sword strapped to his waist to assure us it was he who held the power. He spoke crisply and to the point.

"I am Antonius Antias, and I come in the name of King Herod." He let his pronouncement hang in the air before adding, "On a mission of good will."

"God be with you," Isaac said.

"And who, pray tell, do we intrude upon this evening?" The centurion spoke as if he were merely a vacuum salesman who'd come calling at the front door one sleepy summer evening.

Isaac gestured to his sons and Elisabeth. "I am Isaac, a lowly shepherd, and these are my sons and daughter."

"And you, sir?" The centurion fastened his eyes on me as he leaned forward in his saddle.

"My name is Paul. I'm a friend of the family."

Isaac chimed in. "He has been good enough to help us move our flock to market. To Bethlehem."

The centurion looked around at the flock. "So many shepherds for such a small flock."

"I'm learning," I said. "To be a shepherd. I'm a shepherd in training." I realized how dumb that sounded, but it was already out there. I caught a hint of amusement in Elisabeth's eyes.

The centurion stared at me for a good ten seconds and then smiled. "And where are you good people from?" The Roman's words seemed nonthreatening, but there was an edge in his eyes.

"We live two days' journey to the south and east," Isaac said.

The centurion considered this for a moment. He pointed in the direction from which we'd traveled. "But if you came from hence, wouldn't Jerusalem be a more convenient market?"

An awkward silence followed his question. What was this man getting at? What did he know? Then I remembered a passage from the Gospel of Luke.

And it came to pass in those days, that there went out a decree from Caesar Augustus that all the world should be taxed . . . And all went to be taxed, every one into his own city.

"Bethlehem is my birthplace," I said. "King Herod has decreed that we return home to pay our taxes. And that is why we have chosen Bethlehem as our sheep market."

"What of the rest of you?" the centurion said. "You are not all of Bethlehem."

"We shepherds were born far out in the wilderness," Isaac said. "Therefore we have no city in which to pay our duty to the king. But we will pay our tribute with our friend—tomorrow in Bethlehem—the city of his birth."

I looked up at the gleaming star and wondered why our Roman guests had yet to mention it. Surely they found it as strange and mysterious as we did. Then the familiar voice whispered in my thoughts.

They can't see it.

The star was so clearly there, so obviously real, so . . . brilliant . . . yet it was invisible to Herod's finest. I didn't need the voice to tell me why. I instantly knew. The star was visible only to those with pure motives. For lowly shepherds like us, it was a heavenly guide, showing the way to the Christ child. The light was indiscernible to men such as these, those who held evil intentions in their hearts.

The centurion took a long, thoughtful moment, his gaze resting on Elisabeth. "My men are thirsty and our journey arduous. Perhaps you have wine?"

"We have only what is left from our evening meal," Isaac said. "A small flask of pomegranate that was to last us until we arrive at market."

The centurion nodded to one of his men, who dismounted and went over to Elisabeth. The man held out his hand, and she retrieved the flask and handed it him.

"I hear Bethlehem is filled with wine sellers," the centurion said. "You can purchase more there."

Isaac nodded. I felt my ears turn red. I wanted to knock this guy from his mount and show him how we dealt with thieves back in Brooklyn. The soldier with the wine handed it to Antonius Antias and climbed back onto his mount. The centurion turned up the flask and took a long swig.

"Your wine is quite good," he said.

Isaac nodded.

The commandant wiped his mouth with his sleeve and rolled his head to crack his neck. "Certain rumors have reached the ears of King Herod: rumors of a messiah, a so-called King of the Jews that is to be born in Bethlehem. Have you heard any such talk?"

The centurion's words brought back a troubling memory from boyhood: a Christmas Eve sermon I'd attended with my father the year Mom died. The minister told of Herod's Massacre of the Innocents. I remember crawling under the pew to get away from the horror of it and having nightmares for weeks after. In my dark dream, I'd heard babies crying and mothers screaming and begging for mercy. I always woke up in tears, calling out for my mother. Pops would come in, take me in his arms, and carry me to his room.

"We have heard no such gossip," Isaac said. "We have seen no one to tell us these things."

"What about you?" The Roman centurion looked right at me. I shot a quick glance at Elisabeth. She was watching me closely as if their very lives depended on the next words out of my mouth.

I smiled. "How can a baby be king? There is only one king—that is Herod."

The officer appraised me for a moment before returning my smile. "I'm sure it is nothing but hearsay. However, if you do learn of this baby's whereabouts, we will be in the city. We implore you to tell us what you have found. If there is such a child, Herod wishes to pay tribute." The centurion gripped his reins. "One king to another."

Isaac nodded. "Of course, my lord."

The centurion started to motion his men to leave, then stopped.

"Ah, yes. We encountered travelers along the way who reported seeing an unusual . . . star . . . in the eastern sky." Some of the soldiers broke their icy stares to smile at the absurdity. "Have you seen any such thing as this?"

We all looked up at the magnificent star bathing us in light. I wondered what my companions were thinking.

"No," Teva said. "Only the stars we expect to see."

The centurion nodded. "Perhaps those men had partaken of too much wine." The other soldiers laughed, and we joined them. "Oh, there is one more thing we will need from you before we depart."

"Yes, m'lord?" Isaac said.

"The other shepherds we encountered insisted that we take a lamb from their stock as tribute to the king. I'm sure that you will also be so generous."

I imagined a morning in ninth grade. It was the first day of my freshman year, and I'd been warned about a senior boy named Neal Cantrell, a jock bully who liked to work his way through the freshman boys until he'd tortured each and every one. I'd heard he was already looking for me, so I'd decided there was only one way to deal with the situation.

I found Neal standing by his locker yukking it up with some of his football player buddies. I touched him on the shoulder.

"Neal?"

He had turned toward me and sneered a yellow smile.

"Look, boys. This freshman punk just saved me the trouble of hunting him down."

I'd smiled back and then wiped the taunting grin off his face. Threw him back against the lockers and worked him over as his friends watched in shock.

When he was no longer able to stand, I had nodded to his buddies and calmly walked on to class. I had no trouble from Neal Cantrell or anybody else that year. And there, standing with my shepherd friends, I pictured that moment again, only it was Antonius wearing Neal's letterman jacket. His was the face I was pummeling.

"Take what you will," Isaac said, his voice steeped in sorrow. He knew he had no choice.

Antonius threw up his hand, turned, and galloped off toward Bethlehem, his men following in formation. One of the men diverted to the pasture and plucked a lamb from the flock. We heard its pitiable squeal as he slit its throat, threw it on the back of his mount, and rode off to rejoin his fellow soldiers.

When the Romans were out of range, Aaron picked up a stone and tossed it after them.

"They will find him!" he said. "They will take the child!"

"No," I said. I was surprised at the assurance in my voice. All eyes turned to me. "The same power that kept them from seeing the star will keep the child safe. They won't find him."

I remembered a passage from the Book of Matthew:

And being warned of God in a dream that they should not return to Herod, they departed into their own country another way.

"How can you be so certain?" Teva said.

"I just know," I said. "But something terrible will soon come. They will kill them all. All the baby boys of Bethlehem will be murdered. All but one."

Elisabeth's expression was solemn. She believed me.

Isaac stabbed his crook in the ground. "We cannot wait till morning's light. We must go tonight to Bethlehem. Our king awaits us."

CHAPTER
TWENTY-THREE

We arrived on the outskirts of Bethlehem in the darkest hours before dawn. As he was the youngest, Aaron was tasked with staying with the flock and Elisabeth's burro while the rest of us went into town. Aaron tried to protest, but Isaac hugged his son's neck. "It must be so. Fear not. You will be blessed as we will be blessed."

As we started toward town, Aaron suddenly embraced me. "Before I had yet one brother that I loved. Now I have two." I nodded and put a hand on his shoulder. I felt the same way.

As Isaac, Teva, Elisabeth, and I followed the road into the city, I looked back at him. He met my eye and put a hand over his heart. It seemed almost a gesture of farewell, as if he knew he was never going to see me again.

As we took the final steps into the famed desert town, the star lingered just above the city. I thought again of Pastor Joe and wished he were by my side. I could almost see the gleam in his eye as he watched his Christmas Eve sermon come to life.

"For we saw his star in the east and have come to worship him."

Sunrise was hours away, but the streets of Bethlehem were teeming with travelers. I wasn't sure whether they too had followed the star or were simply there to pay their taxes, but by the looks of them, the latter was true. Many of the travelers were drunken and rowdy, crowding the narrow, dusty thoroughfares until the place felt more like Bourbon Street than Bethlehem. I looked around at the noise and confusion and wondered: how would we ever find one particular stable in the darkness—if there were such a stable at all?

I'd heard the story of Jesus's birth so many times, and in all my imaginings, I'd never pictured Bethlehem like that. Instead of the tranquility of holy night, there were scuffles and fights, and the streets reeked with the near overpowering stench of defecation and decay. The inns were indeed full, and so were the brothels. This unruly desert town seemed an unlikely spot for the Son of God to enter the world.

Among the throng, we spotted the soldiers we'd encountered earlier, holding torches and bullying anyone who stumbled into their path. They were looking for a mother and her newborn boy. The Roman guards, who'd seemed almost gentlemanly with us, were swift and brutal as they strong-armed men, women, and children for information. I watched the imperious Antias lording over it all from his mount. He smiled as one of his soldiers threw an old woman to the ground and kicked her.

Elisabeth turned to me, the fear in her eyes palpable. "I pray the child is not in Bethlehem. Please say that he is not. There is evil here."

I put a hand on her arm. "It's going to be all right. They won't find him."

"How you can know this?" Teva said. "They are turning this place upside down. How can one hide a baby?"

He was right. The town wasn't that big, and there were enough Roman soldiers to tear apart every inch of it. I looked at my friends.

"We'll find the young family in a stable," I said.

Teva chuckled. "The Son of Man born in a lowly animal pen? God would not let it be so."

"No," Elisabeth said. "That is the perfect place. Tell us more, Paul."

Words from Luke, chapter two, verse seven, spilled from my lips. *"And she brought forth her firstborn son, and wrapped him in swaddling clothes, and laid him in a manger; because there was no room for them in the inn.* That's all I know," I said. The New Testament hadn't left a road map.

"This is a prophecy of which you speak?" Isaac said.

I nodded.

"There are many stables," Teva said. "If you do know these things, then please show us which stable, for I fear our time is short."

I looked around. Where to begin? "The stable is attached to some . . . inn. Behind it maybe." I felt helpless. What if the whole story was merely a fabrication, a nice piece of recruiting public relations cooked up by the early Christians? How could I know that the birth really happened in this frenzied place on this night? I looked around for others who might be on the same journey. Where were the wise men and kings? I turned to my friends. They were watching me like helpless children waiting for my direction.

Then, as anxiety and hopelessness again welled up within me, a wind kicked up. It was sudden and strong, a powerful gale that rose full force with no warning. My mind flashed back to the camp and that day by the lake, the afternoon Rebecca plunged headfirst into the storm and into my life. And as if I'd stepped through some invisible door to another moment in time, I was back at the shore on the dark and stormy afternoon at Camp Arrowhead.

"Go read your rule book if you want," the redheaded girl said. "I'm going to go get her."

The wind whistled and howled, and there was Rebecca—so young and freckled and fearless—staring at me, waiting for me to take action.

"So?" she said. "What are you going to do? Are you going to stand on the sidelines or are you going in?"

I heard the voice again. The same voice I'd heard that day, the same voice that was with me in the past.

Go in. Don't be afraid, Paul. I am with you.

As if sucked through some strange wormhole, I was back in Bethlehem. The powerful wind blew through the streets, swirling up dust and blowing all variety of objects in every direction. The mighty gusts extinguished lantern after lantern, torch after torch until the city of Bethlehem was blanketed in total darkness. And where chaos and rancor had been moments before, there was a sudden and striking silence. From the stillness came a troubled hush, punctuated by a few faint cries and whispers, and followed by blind panic. Screaming and crying and fear gripped the brimming desert town. Panic-stricken shadows and shapes ran past us. It was an ominous sign. I felt for Elisabeth's hand.

"Are you all right?" I whispered.

"Yes," she said. Her voice was steady and sure in the dark.

A terrible and overpowering sense of dread overtook me. I sensed that this was the end—that my very existence was about to be wiped clean forever.

I looked up at the star for reassurance, but a black cloud had blown across it, obscuring its light. The comfort the eastern star had brought was gone. There was no peace, no sense of being protected. All the heartbreaking grief over the loss of my daughter and the breakup of my family came rushing back tenfold. My hands began to tremble, and tears streamed from my eyes. I was falling apart. My very being was crumbling.

This must be hell, I thought. All my worst thoughts had returned, and every bit of light and hope had been extinguished from the earth. I wanted to die, to escape that indescribable and soul-crushing feeling. It had all been a scam, a terrible trick. There was no baby, no Christ child, and no hope for humanity. All that I'd experienced in this desert world had simply been an illusion, some strange movie my brain had played as I slowly froze to death in the snow outside Manchester Christian Church. There was no hope for Paul Thomas Bennett. There would be no salvation or redemption. There was only darkness.

And then a face appeared, as if it was floating by in a black void.

I knew it. I knew the face. It was Pastor Joe. He spoke, but his voice was faint and indistinct. His words, though soft and distant, were familiar.

"When you're cast in darkness, there's only one way to go—and that's toward the light." And as the vision of the pastor's face vanished, I played my last desperate card. I closed my eyes and prayed.

God, why have you brought me to this terrible place? Is it because I'm unworthy?

Immediately, the voice responded.

Fear thou not; for I am with thee: be not dismayed; for I am thy God: I will strengthen thee; yea, I will help thee; yea, I will uphold thee with the right hand of my righteousness.

I felt as if two invisible arms reached out and wrapped me in a bear hug embrace. The hopeless despair that threatened to swallow me whole was eased. The voice came again, only this time the words spilled from my own lips.

"You are my lamp, O Lord; the Lord turns my darkness into light."

In the heavens above, the clouds slowly rolled back to—once again—reveal the brilliant star of Bethlehem. And though the chaos of fear and confusion continued to swirl about us, I again felt peace. The voice and the star's light had chased away my dark thoughts.

Elisabeth touched my arm. "Paul? What is it?"

I looked at her and smiled. "I think I know where to look! I think I know where to find the baby."

I found a wooden ladder leaning against a nearby building and scurried up to the roof.

From my precarious perch, I could see the entire dark city. I scanned every direction searching and seeking and then . . . I spotted it. The beam from a dim lantern illuminated a tiny corner of the desert town, its soft glow beckoning like a miniature lighthouse. The only lantern that was still burning.

There was one light left in Bethlehem.

I called back down to my friends.

"I've found our stable."

CHAPTER
TWENTY-FOUR

Our band of four followed the faint light to the stoop of a nonde-
script little inn. There was a crude sign on the door: "No room." As we
approached, a small barrel-shaped man with a tuft of untidy white hair
swung the door open and glared at us, a dirty lantern dangling from
his fingers.

"What do you want?" he said. "Can't you read the sign?"

"Do you have a stable?" I said.

"Why does that matter to you? You have no animals."

For some reason, I found him amusing. This bit player in the nativity story was exactly as I had pictured him.

Elisabeth smiled at the man. "We are looking for friends. We think
they might be in your stable."

The stubby man glared at her. "My stable seems to be popular
tonight. For what reason, I know not." He cocked his head to the left.
"Around back. Tell them I want them cleared out by first light. And it
better be left like they found it!" And with that, he slammed the door
in our faces.

Between the inn and the next building was a tight alley, a passage-
way barely wide enough for a man to slip through. Down the narrow

way, I could see the glow of a lantern casting shadows on the dingy walls. I looked back at the others, nodded toward the opening, and guided them in.

I was first to emerge on the other side and was sure we'd come to the wrong place. Maybe we were looking for some other inn. The little stable was so small—a tiny sagging stall in desperate need of repair. Could this really contain the manger of legend?

But, on that night of nights, the shepherds were by no means the first to arrive. Already on hand were wise men, kings, and ordinary peasants—nearly two dozen travelers had found their way to this crowded little shed on that holy night. They were facing away from us, gathered in a semicircle and blocking my view of whatever had so captured their attention.

I looked back at my friends. They were watching me with amused looks as if I'd walked in on my own surprise party, and they were in on it all along.

"What?" I said to Elisabeth. Her nod toward the gathered told me *Go on. What are you waiting for?*

I was suddenly taken with how ordinary it all seemed. Where were the trumpets and angels, the heavenly host? This wasn't at all how I'd pictured it. There was no painting or drawing or rendering I'd ever seen that portrayed the nativity in this fashion. I looked up through the cavernous hole in the roof, and there it was—winking down at me like an old friend. The Christmas star hovered at twelve o'clock. I felt the warmth of its beam as it bathed me in its strange and wonderful light. The majestic star was speaking to me, whispering right into my soul.

This is what you've been searching for, Paul. You've come home.

As I cautiously stepped into the stall, my fellow travelers parted like waves of grain. Wise men, kings, and peasants turned, watching me pass as if they were merely background characters in a play written solely for my benefit.

And then . . . there they were: mother, father, and babe—a humble family of three nestled against the back of the stall, a tuft of hay in a wooden feeding trough for a crib.

The manger.

My eyes rested on the Christ child wrapped in a swaddle. The baby was awake and looking up at his mother. His eyes were smiling, and the light from the star glanced off his soft cheeks and forehead. His little hands were moving, conducting some invisible choir. Dad Joseph was kneeling behind mother and child, a hand on Mary's shoulder, gazing lovingly at his newborn son.

I was puzzled at first and couldn't quite believe what I was witnessing, and then, all at once, my legs turned to taffy. The feeling was so strong and sudden . . . a sensation that I can only describe as an intense and overwhelming humility. The word "meekness" came to mind, and I'd never really understood what the word meant until that moment. I sank to my knees and buried my face in my hands.

I shouldn't be here, I thought. *I'm not worthy to see this.*

A tremendous sense of shame washed over me as I thought about all the bitterness and resentment that had grown like a cancer inside me. I was selfish and sinful and ungrateful, and I did not belong there. I wanted to turn and run away, to get as far away from this stable as my legs would carry me. I wanted to flee, to escape the feeling that had gripped me, but I couldn't move. My will had surrendered to an infinitely greater power, and I'd lost control of myself. The walls of resistance collapsed.

I sobbed unashamedly. I cried like I hadn't cried since I was a little boy, perhaps like I'd never cried before. I cried tears of contrition and regret and relief. I cried with my whole shuddering body. I cried until I was sure there were no tears left in my ducts and then somehow more came. I cried until I felt a gentle touch on my shoulder, stirring me from my weeping.

I looked up into Elisabeth's angelic face.

"She's calling for you," she said. Her voice was soft and sure, and she didn't seem the least bit impressed or put off by my outpouring of grief.

Mary was smiling at me. The young mother's nod beckoned me to come and have a look. I knew her request was impossible to fulfill. I didn't have the strength. My wobbly, undeserving legs wouldn't support my weight. I had no muscle memory and couldn't even stand up. But then Elisabeth held out her hand, and when I took it I felt a surge of energy. My strength had returned.

I stood and looked around at the others. All eyes were fixed on me, patiently waiting. Their faces were kind and patient, as if they had all the time in the world.

I took the five faltering steps to where the child lay. With my body trembling, my chin quivering, I knelt in front of the manger. I had no idea what one was supposed to say or do at such a moment in history. Tears streamed down my cheeks as I gazed on the baby Jesus. And at that moment—as I looked on that sweet, innocent face—nothing else in the world mattered. Nothing at all. I had no past and no future. There was nothing within or without. There was only that moment and that child. He *knew* me. He knew everything there was to know about me—all the good and bad, all my secrets and fears. And I knew that he knew, and I felt no shame.

The baby smiled, and a rush of light flowed through me. And there was a great change. I was instantly transformed. With that one little smile, this newborn baby dissolved every trace of sorrow, regret, hatred, and self-loathing from my life. And they weren't just *gone*—those dark traits had never existed, as though I'd dreamed them and now had been awakened to realize they'd never been real at all.

I was redeemed.

Something small and heavy appeared on my chest, and I looked down. There, hanging about my neck, was the little ring necklace Abbey had left me for Christmas, the same pitiful ring I'd once given Rebecca on that crisp, cold New Year's Eve in Central Park. I'd always thought of it as a poor substitute for a diamond. But as I cupped it in my hand there by the manger, I realized that this unassuming necklace was the true diamond, the meek symbol of a love that had changed my life. Rebecca Anne Waverly was the love of my life. But she wasn't separate from me; we were one, and we always would be.

I turned my gaze from the sparkling charm in my hand to the new family before me. I removed the necklace and carefully placed it among the other gifts of frankincense, gold, and myrrh. It was a simple yet heartfelt offering, and it was all I had to give.

Mary and Joseph exchanged a smile. They seemed to approve of my humble gift.

I stood and stepped aside to allow the kings and wise men and shepherds, each in turn, to place their offerings on the makeshift altar. As I watched the scene that I'd long ago imagined as a boy sitting beside my mother in church on Christmas Eve, I suddenly felt detached from it all, as if I were looking into a snow globe.

"Paul."

I turned to find Elisabeth standing beside me. She took my face in her soft hands and gazed into my eyes.

"It's time for you to go home," she said.

The idea seemed ridiculous. Why would I want to go anywhere? This was where I wanted to be, where I needed to be. I finally felt contentment. I was finally home.

"But I don't want to leave," I said. "My life back there—it has no meaning to me anymore. It doesn't seem real. Please. I want to stay here with you and the others. It all makes sense to me now. For the first time, life makes sense. *I* make sense. I can't go back now. I'm afraid that if I go, I'll lose this feeling and never get it back."

Elisabeth smiled. "Oh, Paul. You won't lose this gift. You can never lose it." She put her hand over my heart. "It's in here forever. Paul, don't you see?"

"I don't understand," I said. "Why? Why me?" I felt my knees weaken again. I held on to her to keep my balance.

"Because you are worthy, Paul. Because God loves you more than you know."

"If this is . . . a *gift*," I said, "then who is it . . . from?"

Elisabeth didn't answer. Instead, she smiled, nodding to a young girl who was bowing before the baby Jesus, her back to us, her head shrouded in a scarf. The scarf was deep maroon and old and woolen and tattered. I knew that scarf.

"What?" I said. "Who is she?"

I watched the girl place her gift near Mary's feet. Then she stood and turned to me, and as she did, she pulled the ragged scarf from her head, letting her scarlet hair spill down over her shoulders. It was my old scarf, the same one Rebecca had brought to my room that night in Brooklyn when she broke my window and mended my heart. The same scarf Megan had worn that Christmas morning when she ran off to Waller's Pond to try out her new white-leather skates.

It was Megan. *My* Megan. She was alive!

She was older, maybe thirteen or fourteen, but I knew her in an instant. She had the same sweet face and smile and eyes. My daughter was standing before me, and she looked . . . perfect.

"Megan . . ." I said. I could scarcely grasp what I was seeing. How could this be? How could she be there with me? Then again, how could any of it be?

The girl that was my daughter smiled at me, and then came over and took my hands. The touch was familiar, the feel of her skin, the smell of her. It was Megan. She was real: alive and real. Of that I had no doubt.

"Merry Christmas, Daddy."

For a moment, I couldn't remember how to make my tongue form syllables. There was so much I wanted to say, yet I didn't remember how talking worked.

"Meggy . . . I miss you so much."

"I know. But I'll see you again someday . . . a long time from now. And we'll take a walk together in the woods. We'll go skating."

Megan was there with me, and it was strange and wonderful and miraculous. I wanted to tell her things. So many things. I wanted to let her know how much I missed her, how I thought about her every moment of every day. But as my already teetering knees began to wobble, she simply smiled as if she didn't need me to tell her a thing.

"I know, Daddy. I know."

Dizziness hit me full force, and I was spinning on an out-of-control merry-go-round. Megan's face grew blurry. I was going to pass out. I desperately tried to stay focused, to stay there with her, but an uncontrollable trembling took over my body. My knees and arms and teeth quaked violently, as if I were about to split apart at the seams. I struggled to stay awake; I needed to stay with Megan. There was so much to say . . . to tell her. But I couldn't fight it. I'd lost all control.

"Megan . . ." I said once more and sank to the ground. Through a haze, a vague image of my little girl looked down at me. She was smiling and didn't seem to be the least bit concerned about my troubling condition. When she spoke, her voice sounded far off.

"It's all right, Daddy. You're going to be okay."

The ground opened up and I fell, down, down into a black well: a dark and narrow void of indefinable size and dimension. The light moved away, growing dimmer and smaller and more distant, until I was enveloped in total blackness.

CHAPTER
TWENTY-FIVE

Where was I? What was happening? As I moved deeper and deeper into the dark and mysterious abyss, I felt helpless. Alone. I strained to see, to make out something, but the blackness was all encompassing, like I was in a deep and endless cave far below the earth's surface where not even a hint of light could talk its way in.

Then came another voice. It wasn't the voice I'd heard in my head, the voice that had been with me during my time in the past. It was a deep voice, rich and soothing and . . . familiar. The words were faint but quickly grew more distinct, as if I were moving nearer and nearer to the source.

"Son, are you all right? Hello?"

A flicker of light appeared, a tiny point far in front of me. That's when I realized I wasn't falling backward at all. I was moving forward, and as I did, the light grew brighter and brighter. Pastor Joe's words echoed in my mind. "When you're cast in darkness, there's only one way to go—and that's into the light."

"You okay, young fella?"

The bodiless voice was now so close I could nearly touch it.

"Do you need me to call 911?"

I'd stopped moving. I was completely still, and my eyes slowly focused. As the vague images in front of me took shape, my first sensation was of biting cold.

Snowflakes swirled down on me, settling on my cheeks and nose and mouth. As rational thought again took hold, I realized I was flat on my back. My lips were chapped from the brisk night air. I looked up into the eyes of an old man. The face was lined and wise and oh so familiar. Even in his winter coat and top hat, the dapper old fella looked a good bit like a certain shepherd I once knew. Isaac.

"Here, let me give you a hand," the man said. He held out his arm, and I took it. I thought that he was strong for a man his age as he helped me to my feet.

I dusted off the snow as I took in my surroundings. I was home again. Manchester, Maine: circa the present. I was standing outside my old church, and it was snowing. In the steeple above the street, ol' Walter rang the bell, the peals echoing into the wintry night. It was eight o'clock, and people were arriving for the Christmas Eve service. Pastor Joe would be there, and he'd be reading the familiar story of a curious star that hovered over an ancient desert town called Bethlehem. He'd tell again of mother and father and baby, of wise men and kings and shepherds—all gathered in a stable, on a long-ago night, around a manger.

It was a simple story, one that had been told so many times before.

It was a story of love and hope and salvation.

The greatest story ever told.

"Must have hit your head," the man said. I gave him a confused look. "On the curb," he said. "Must have slipped and hit your head on the curb."

I remembered hitting my head, but it felt so long ago. Days. Weeks. Or was it? I touched the back of my scalp. No bump. Not even a bit sore.

"I seem to be okay," I said.

"Well, good," the gentleman said. "In that case, I think I'll head inside for the Christmas Eve service. I like to arrive early so I can get a good seat." The familiar gent tipped his hat and called out "Merry Christmas" as he headed inside the church.

I looked around for my postal bag, but it was nowhere to be found. What could have happened to it? Then I noticed what I was wearing. I was no longer in my everyday postal blues; I was decked out in my Sunday best Kenneth Cole suit. The suit I hadn't worn in four years—not since Megan's funeral.

Then, in my head, I heard the familiar voice once again.

If thou canst believe, all things are possible to him that believeth.

I turned and ran home, slipping and sliding like George Bailey through Bedford Falls, past the shops and stores and houses I'd come to know so well. Somewhere in my gut, I knew they would be there. As I jogged along the icy streets, I could scarcely feel the ground beneath my feet. I was euphoric and giddy, and filled with a hope and joy so overpowering I felt I could break free from the confines of gravity and float away, up past the light poles and tree branches and rooftops up and up and up into the night sky.

As I rounded the corner onto our street, I stopped in my tracks and caught my breath. My heart sank. The house at 25 Bethlehem Place was dark. Our home looked forlorn and forgotten.

I walked slowly down the block like a little boy approaching a haunted house. I stopped at our front gate beside the mailbox that said "The Bennetts." My hopes waned. I had come home to an empty house.

As I started to turn away, a porch light flicked on. A moment later, another light appeared in the living-room window and then another in the den, and then another and another until the Bennett family home was beaming like a lighthouse guiding a ship back to port.

"Paul?"

I hadn't even noticed the front door open, but there she stood. She was in shadow, framed by the glowing house behind her. And then she took a step into the light.

Elisabeth! I thought. No, it wasn't Elisabeth. It was Rebecca. Both shared the same heart-shaped face, the same luminous auburn hair and sparkling hazel eyes. I knew then that Elisabeth and Rebecca, Rebecca and Elisabeth, were one and the same. My beloved wife and friend had been with me the whole time.

She hugged her arms across her chest and shivered.

"You need to get back inside," I said. "It's the rules."

Rebecca looked at me warily, and I wondered if she remembered our first words so many years ago in a rainstorm by the lake at Camp Arrowhead. I sensed she was being cautious, as if expecting my good cheer to evaporate like a mirage.

"Go read your rule book if you want," she said testing the waters.

I stepped up to the edge of the steps and just looked at her, drinking her in as if I hadn't laid eyes on her in a long, long time. "You came home," I said.

She averted her gaze. "Christmas is family time. Despite everything, you still are a part of this family."

"Becca, I'm so sorry. Can you ever forgive—"

"Shhh." She put a finger to her lips and studied my face. As she peered into my eyes, I had the distinct impression she was trying to make sure I wasn't some imposter parading around in her husband's body. "Paul?" Becca finally said, her voice an involuntary whisper, as if she'd just opened the door to a long lost friend.

"Yeah," I said. "It's me."

She reached up to touch my face, but stopped short and took a step back. "Before I let you pass through this door, I must ask you one question."

"Anything," I said.

"How much do you love me?"

My eyes welled up with tears, and a lump came to my throat. "More than life. I love you more than life."

Rebecca's eyes filled, and she held out her hand. I took it and thought how warm and welcoming it felt. I lifted her off the porch and into my arms. I spun her around and kissed her, and when I opened my eyes, it seemed the weather had changed on cue—the gentle fall of snow had picked up, scattering snowflakes in her hair and eyelashes and on the warm curve of her cheeks, which were flushed with the cold. And when I put her down, she smiled and mouthed the most beautiful four words ever known to man.

"I love you, too."

"Mommy, Daddy! Look what I found!" Abbey burst through the front door, calling out as if the fact she was speaking for the first time in years was the most natural thing in the world. "Isn't it cool?"

Rebecca and I exchanged a look. We wanted to react, wanted to shout our gratitude to the heavens, but instead, we followed our little girl's cue. We acted as if the sudden return of Abbey's voice was simply to be expected. After all, it was Christmas, and Christmas is the season of miracles. But it wasn't until I noticed a splash of color on her coat that I realized what she was so excited about. There, draped around her neck, was that old all-too-familiar maroon scarf. "I found it on my bed," she said. "On my pillow. Did you put it there, Daddy?"

Rebecca glanced at me, perhaps suspecting I might be Abbey's secret Santa.

"Not me," I said.

Abbey affectionately rubbed the woolen fabric. "Can I keep it?"

"Sure, why not?" I said. "Whoever put it there must have wanted you to have it."

"Okay," Rebecca said with an easy smile, as if she'd set down a heavy load she'd been carrying for far too long. "We'd better go get ready."

"Ready?" I asked.

"Church. We don't want to miss Pastor Joe's Christmas Eve sermon." She put a hand on the lapel of my suit. "Looks like you're fine as you are."

As if on cue, Walter began to ring the old church bell, just like he'd done thousands of times before. Soon, doors all over town would swing open, and families would step into the cold December night and join with others making their way to the glowing little church on the square.

Rebecca, Abbey, and I joined hands and began our walk through the snow, ready to hear a young minister—who had found his own way through the dark—tell of a long-ago night when wise men and kings and shepherds followed a glorious Christmas star to a new beginning in a little town called Bethlehem.

ACKNOWLEDGMENTS

I've now written enough Christmas movies and novels that I consider myself something of a St. Nicholas Sparks. Yes, Christmas has been, up to now, a very important part of my life and career. And it all started with that extraordinary story I first heard as a miniature Sunday school student at a small church in western North Carolina so many Decembers ago. In my humble opinion, the original Christmas story is not only the greatest story ever told, but also one of the most compelling. And each time I hear or read it, I find myself gravitating to those humble shepherds. Did they really know how fortunate they were? What were their lives like before and after they took part in the very first Christmas? I wonder what it would have been like to travel with them, a fellow journeyman on hand to bear witness to this seminally important moment in human history. And though I can't actually realize that dream, I thought (at least) I could write about a man who did: an ordinary modern man with challenges and hard times not unlike myself. Hence, *The Christmas Star* was born.

This story is about redemption and love and gratitude, and I am profoundly grateful to those who have shepherded (so to speak) this novel from a kernel of an idea to publication. I must begin with my own parents (especially my mother), both of whom are no longer with us, but who read this story in its original short form and said they thought it held promise. I'd like to give thanks for my tireless and supremely talented agent, Jessica Kirkland, for believing in me and this book. I'm grateful I know you.

I'd like to give a gratitude "shout out" to Acquisitions Editor (and Manchester, Maine's favorite daughter) Erin Mooney at Amazon Publishing's Waterfall Press for seeing something in this book that she liked and bringing it into the Amazon fold. I'm grateful to Brooklyn's own Andrew Pantoja, a skilled and patient editor who enabled me to see this novel through a fresh pair of eyes and helped me find the way to bring it home. I'd also like to give my heartfelt appreciation to our cover designer, Shasti O'Leary Soudant, for a truly lovely and creative book cover, and to the novel's skilled developmental editor, Leslie Lutz, and copyeditor, Laura Whittemore, for their keen eyes and careful attention to detail.

I'm also so deeply grateful for the many friends and family members who have so richly populated my days and years. There are pieces and parts of each of you in the characters that make up this story. Your love and support is among my life's greatest gifts.

Lastly, and most importantly, I must express my gratitude and love to God for guidance and direction. That wonderfully simple statement in the Book of Proverbs pretty much sums it up. *Trust in the Lord with all thine heart; and lean not unto thine own understanding. In all thy ways acknowledge him, and he shall direct thy paths.*

ABOUT THE AUTHOR

Photo © 2017 Bob Lovett

Born in Atlanta, Georgia, Robert Tate Miller was raised in the North Carolina mountain town of Hendersonville, where his family moved when he was three. Rob's family was in the hotel business, and at age eleven, he had his first job—taking reservations, busing tables, cutting grass, and caring for the pool and shuffleboard courts. Rob started writing for fun around that time and grew up to become a professional writer, selling the first of many published essays to the *Christian Science Monitor* in 1994. He went on to write numerous screenplays and has seen five of his movies make it to the small screen. His TV movie credits include *Three Days*, *Secret Santa*, *Hidden Places*, *Farewell Mr. Kringle*, and *Christmas Cookies*, and he also wrote the novels *Secret Santa* (Atria) and *Forever Christmas* (Thomas Nelson).

Rob graduated from East Henderson High School and attended the University of Georgia, where he earned a BA in journalism/mass communications. He has also worked as a studio cameraman, a game show producer, a TV promotions writer/producer, a teacher, a college student house manager, and an editor, as well as in media relations. He lives in Northridge, California.